*Being as how Brooke Fallon Grant was his buddy Cory's sister and his buddy Cory being a pretty good-looking guy, he hadn't been expecting a troll.*

But the woman standing before him …well, the only word that suited her was *lovely*.

Tony had a photographer's eye, of course, one that saw beyond the fatigue lines, no makeup and hair that was limp and dull and in need of washing. What he saw was dark blue eyes that told you they'd seen more than they wanted to of the world's sadness and suffering. And amazing bones, the kind that made him itch to reach for his camera. Which was too bad, because he was pretty sure the first time he aimed a lens in the lady's direction she'd sic her monster dog on him.

*At the very least.* He'd forgotten for a moment he might be looking at the face of a cold-blooded killer.

Dear Reader,

I hope you're enjoying the series THE TAKEN, which tells of *Secret Agent Sam* hero Cory Pearson's search for his lost siblings. When I wrote my introductory letter for the series, I mentioned that it had personal meaning for me. Now, I can tell you of an amazing thing that has happened in my life. During the writing of this book, I made contact with my own "lost" siblings. Life is a series of miracles, isn't it?

*Lady Killer* is the third book in the series. The first two books were Cory's brothers' stories. In this book and the next—the fourth and final chapter coming next month—it's the girls' turn: twin sisters, separated not only from the brothers they never knew, but, thanks to unspeakable events in their childhood, from each other. Come with us now and share their journey as they struggle to overcome great odds and find lasting love, and at the same time rediscover each other and the brothers lost so many years ago....

Enjoy!

*Kathleen Creighton*

# KATHLEEN CREIGHTON

*Lady Killer*

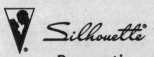

Romantic
SUSPENSE

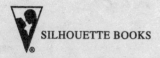

SILHOUETTE BOOKS

Recycling programs
for this product may
not exist in your area.

ISBN-13: 978-0-373-27629-5
ISBN-10:    0-373-27629-X

LADY KILLER

Copyright © 2009 by Kathleen Creighton-Fuchs

**Printed in U.S.A.**

**Books by Kathleen Creighton**

## KATHLEEN CREIGHTON

has roots deep in the California soil but has relocated to South Carolina. As a child, she enjoyed listening to old timers' tales, and her fascination with the past only deepened as she grew older. Today, she says she is interested in everything—art, music, gardening, zoology, anthropology and history, but people are at the top of her list. She also has a lifelong passion for writing, and now combines her two loves in romance novels.

For Tom and Deb, Bob and Melodie
whose acceptance and love enrich my life
beyond measure.

# Prologue

*In a house on the shores of a small lake somewhere in South Carolina...*

"Pounding—that's always the first thing. Someone—my father—is banging on the door. Banging...pounding...with his fists, feet, I don't know. Trying to break it down."

"And...where are *you?*"

"I'm in a bedroom, I think. I don't remember which one. I have the little ones with me. It's my job to look after them when my father is having one of his...spells. I have to keep them out of his way. Keep them safe. I've taken them into the bedroom, and I've locked the door, except...I don't trust the lock, so I've wedged a chair under the handle, like my mom showed me. Only…now I'm afraid…terrified even that won't be enough. I can hear the wood splintering…breaking. I know it will only take a few more blows and he'll be through. My mother is screaming…crying. I hold on to the little ones…I have my arms around them, and they're all trembling. The twins, the little girls, are sobbing and crying, 'Mama, Mama…' but the boys just cry quietly.

"I hear sirens…more sirens, getting louder and louder, until it seems they're coming right into the room, and there's lots of people shouting…and all of a sudden the pounding stops. There's a moment…several minutes…when all I hear is the little ones whimpering…and then there's a loud bang, so loud we—the children and I—all jump. We hold each other tighter, and there's another bang, and we flinch again, and then there's just confusion…voices shouting…footsteps running…glass breaking…the little ones crying…and I think I might be crying, too.…"

He discovered he *was* crying, but he also knew it was all right. *He* was all right. Sam, his wife, was holding him tightly, cradling his head against her breasts, and her hands were gentle as they wiped the tears from his face.

"I'm going to find them, Sam. My brothers and sisters. I have to find them."

Samantha felt warm moisture seep between her lashes. "Of course, you do." She lifted her head and took her husband's face between her hands and smiled fiercely at him through her tears. "We'll find them together, Pearse," she whispered. "We'll find them. I promise you we will."

# Chapter 1

The black SUV was parked just off the main road on the rocky dirt track that ran around the back side of Brooke's twenty-five acres. Not far enough off the road to be hidden by the live oaks that grew thickly there, so she couldn't help but see it as she slowed for her driveway a hundred yards farther on. She didn't need to see the license plate to know who the SUV belonged to, and the knowledge sent a shock wave of fury through her. There could be only one reason for that car being parked where it was.

Duncan was spying on her.

The cold, clutching feeling in her stomach was one she'd come to know well in the months since Duncan had filed for custody of Daniel. Although the divorce had been no picnic, she'd never been afraid, not *then*. Only relieved. But that had been before she'd had to consider the unthinkable: the possibility that she could lose Daniel.

*I can't lose Daniel. Duncan Grant is* not *taking my son*.

She wouldn't have thought such a thing could happen, never in a million years. She was a good mother. She owned her own ranch—twenty-five acres' worth, tiny by Texas standards, but at least it was paid for—and thanks to the untimely death of her parents in a freeway pileup two years ago, she was also independently well-off. But this was still a good ol' boy's county, and Duncan being a deputy sheriff, he had powerful allies. And now, thanks to that idiot at the feed store who'd lost her order, Duncan might actually have that ammunition he'd been looking for in his battle to win custody of their son.

Because of the delay at the feed store, she was late getting home. Daniel would have been home alone for at least an hour, and although Brooke knew he was an exceptionally responsible child and quite capable of taking care of himself for that period of time, she feared a judge would consider only the fact that he was nine years old and disregard any mitigating circumstances.

Damn Duncan, anyway. How could he have managed to show up unannounced on the one day it mattered? He wasn't due to have Daniel until next weekend. How had he known? Unless—her stomach clenched again— unless one of his buddies had happened to see her truck in town and had reported it to him. It was the kind of thing Duncan would do, set his network of good ol' boys to spying on her for him.

Then she thought, Oh, Brooke, you're being paranoid.

But the thought came creeping back: why else would he be here, lurking on the back lane?

All that rocketed through her mind in a matter of seconds while she closed the distance between the lane and her mailbox, and her heart was tripping along faster than it ought to and the coldness was sitting in her belly as she turned into her driveway. The coldness spread all through her as she drove past the live oaks that surrounded her house and the accompanying assortment of outbuildings and animal enclosures that qualified the property as a ranch.

*Where in the world is Hilda? And Daniel?*

Normally, the Great Pyrenees—Duncan had given the huge dog, then only an adorable fur ball, to Daniel on his fifth birthday—would come bounding out to meet her, giddy with joy at her return, with Daniel not far behind. But the lane remained empty, and there was still no sign of either child or shaggy white-and-fawn dog as Brooke circled the house and drove across the yard to the barn and the feed storage shed next to it. The place seemed deserted.

That is, until she turned off the motor and opened the door. Then the noise hit her. Hilda's frantic barking. And something else. Something that made the hair prickle on the back of her neck: the unmistakable scream of an angry cougar.

Whispering—whimpering— "OhGodohGodohGod, please, God…no…" under her breath, Brooke tumbled out of the pickup and raced through the open middle of the barn. Out the back and down the lane between the animal pens she ran, not even aware of her feet touching the ground. The cougar's screaming and Hilda's barking grew louder as she ran, filling her head, filling her with a fear so terrible, she couldn't think, couldn't feel, could barely even see.

What she did see, as if through the wrong end of a telescope, was Hilda, lunging frantically at the gate to the wire-enclosed compound far down at the end of the lane and barking with frustration at her inability to get past the high chain-link barricade. Brooke felt a momentary surge of relief, followed by an even more desperate fear.

*Lady—thank God! She's not loose, after all! But—oh, God—where is Daniel? Oh, my God—Daniel!*

Her son was nowhere in sight, but for Hilda to be so upset, he had to be here. Which could only mean one thing. He was *inside* the cougar's compound.

*But why?* Although she and Daniel had raised the cougar together from a tiny kitten, the boy knew very well Lady wasn't a pet, that she was a wild predator and could never be trusted. Daniel would never go into her cage. Not alone. He just *wouldn't*.

But he had. She could hear him now, his voice quavering and breathless one moment, firm and commanding the next. *And he sounds so very, very young.*

Shouting, sobbing "No—no, Lady—*back*. Lady—*back!*"

Sobbing herself now, Brooke reached the cougar's enclosure, and gripping the wire with both hands, she stared in disbelief at the scene beyond the fence. Daniel, with his back to her, *her child,* holding a rake aloft like a battle sword and a folded saddle blanket over his other arm like a shield, facing down a full-grown mountain lion. And the lion, teeth bared, screaming and snarling in fury as she backed slowly toward the door to her holding cage, pausing now to swipe at the air with her claws.

"Daniel!" His name felt ripped from her throat by forces outside herself.

He didn't turn, but she heard his breathless "I'm okay, Mom."

At that moment the cougar, for whatever reason— perhaps returned to sanity from whatever terrible place she'd been by the voice of the only mother she'd ever known?—gave one last huffing growl, turned and sprang through the door and into her cage. Daniel scrambled after her to throw the bar across the door. By that time Brooke had opened the gate to the compound and was there to catch him when he turned, sobbing, into her arms.

But he'd only let himself stay there a moment, of course, being all too mindful of the fact that he was the man in their household now. For the space of a couple of deep, shuddering breaths, he gripped her tightly, arms wrapped around her waist, and allowed her to smooth his sweat-soaked hair with her own shaking hands. Then he let go, stepped back and wiped his face with a quick swipe of a forearm, leaving a smear of mud across one hot red cheek.

"She didn't mean to, Mom. I know she didn't mean to." His words came rapidly, choked and breathless with his efforts to hold the tears at bay.

"Daniel, honey, what—" She reached for him, but he took another step back, eluding her, and shook his head with a heartbreaking desperation.

"She didn't mean to hurt him. I know she didn't."

"Honey, hurt *who?* What are you—"

"It's Dad." He grew still, with a calm that was somehow more frightening than the tears. He drew a deep breath and brushed once more at his damp cheeks. "I think he's dead, Mom." His eyes moved, looking past her.

Biting back another question, Brooke instead jerked herself around to follow his gaze and saw what she hadn't before, when her entire focus had been on her son and the cougar. Saw what looked like a pile of tumbled rags lying a little farther along the base of the chain-link fence.

She stared at it, shock numbing her mind, paralyzing her body, so that for a moment she didn't register what she was seeing. Then she couldn't believe what she was seeing. Couldn't let herself believe. The unthinkable.

Not rags, but clothing. A man's clothing—jeans and a tan-colored shirt. With blood on them. Scuffed cowboy boots turned at an odd angle. And a brown Stetson, the kind the sheriff's deputies wore. She knew that Stetson. She knew those boots.

She didn't know how long she stood there, unable to move, unable to think. Then Daniel moved, started toward the body—for that's what it undeniably was—on the ground, and she reached out and grabbed hold of his arm and pulled him back. "No, no, honey. Don't—" Her voice broke.

"But what if he needs help? What if he's—"

Brooke just shook her head. She simply couldn't make any more words come out of her mouth.

Then, from far off in the distance, she heard sirens.

Daniel heard them, too, and caught a quick breath,

his face seeming to brighten with hope. "I called nine-one-one. I bet that's them. Maybe it's the paramedics. They'll help him, won't they, Mom?"

Hearing the anguish in her son's voice, seeing the entreaty in his dark blue eyes, Brooke felt a measure of calm come to take the place of the shock that had kept her frozen and numb. She took her son by his shoulders—small shoulders, a child's shoulders, too small to bear such a burden—and held him tightly and with a terrible urgency so that he had to look at her. "Daniel, quick, before they get here, tell me what happened. How did this happen? How did he—"

"I don't know, Mom." His eyes grew bright, almost glassy, whether with shock or more tears, Brooke didn't know. "I got home from school and you weren't here, so I came in the house and got an ice-cream sandwich out of the freezer, because I was hungry. And then I heard Hilda barking. And she kept barking and barking. And I thought maybe something was wrong, and you weren't here, so I went out to see, and I brought the cell phone, like you told me."

The sirens were louder now, coming along the road, almost to the driveway. She gave Daniel's shoulders another shake. "Yes, yes, and…"

"And I saw Dad lying there, inside Lady's pen. I don't know how he got in there, Mom, I swear. I didn't leave the gate unlocked."

"Never mind that now. And Lady?"

"She was there, too, sort of crouched down beside… him. She had blood on her—you know, on her paws and stuff. When she saw me, she started snarling and screaming. I never saw her like that before, Mom. I didn't know what to do, so I called nine-one-one. Then I thought maybe he was—maybe Dad was…you know, still alive. So that's when I got the rake and started making her get away from him. She didn't try to attack me or anything, Mom, I swear. It was like she was just really upset. I know she didn't mean to hurt Dad. She wouldn't."

The last words were shouted above the noise of the sirens, which had risen to a deafening crescendo before dying away to a series of wails as the emergency vehicles—several, by the sound of them—pulled one after another into the yard.

Brooke gripped Daniel's shoulders harder. "Listen, don't say anything. I'll handle this. Let me handle it, okay?"

Daniel sniffed and nodded, but his eyes were filled with fear, probably the same fear that was in Brooke's heart. He put both their fears into words, in a very small voice. "They aren't going to kill her, are they? You won't let them kill her." They both knew what happened to animals who turned on their human keepers.

She shook her head and clamped her teeth together, tightening her jaws as she turned to face the fire department paramedics who were just coming through the barn, coming at a rapid jog-trot.

"In here! He's in here."

She opened the gate and held it as the EMTs—a young man she didn't know and a woman she knew from church, a heavyset Hispanic girl named Rosie—brushed past her. As she watched them kneel beside the body and immediately check for a pulse, Brooke reached for

Daniel and pulled him against her, held him snug against her front, with her arms crisscrossing his chest. She could feel him trembling and realized she was, too.

Then time seemed to slow, and it seemed a very long time passed while she watched the two EMTs bending over the body of the man she'd once loved, once shared a bed with, still shared a child with…watched them calmly and methodically going about their business, all of them knowing it was pointless but going through with it, anyway. That strange and dreamlike feeling persisted until she heard heavy footsteps and half-turned and took a step back to make room for the sheriff's deputies who were just arriving, and her heart sank when she saw one of them was Duncan's partner, Lonnie Doyle.

Of course, it would be Lonnie. This was going to hit him hard.

"Dunk? Ah, no—ah, jeez! Ah, hell—"

Lonnie had barreled past her and gotten close enough to what was lying on the ground being worked on by the EMTs to see who it was, and that whatever the medics were doing, it wasn't going to be enough. She'd unconsciously braced herself but winced anyway when he jerked to a halt, then whirled on her, his fleshy face red with rage.

"What the hell did you *do?* How did this happen? It was that damned cat, wasn't it? That cat killed him— killed my partner!" His hand was at his waist, gripping the handle of his weapon. "Hell, I'm gonna take care of this right now! Right here!"

"No—it wasn't—" Brooke began in a desperate gasp as Daniel uttered a wounded cry and tore himself away from her, hurled himself at the cougar's cage and spread-eagled himself across the door.

"It wasn't Lady's fault! It was mine. I did something to make her mad. She didn't mean—"

"No—it was an accident. Just an accident. That's all." Breathless with fear, Brooke planted herself between her son and the man bent on exacting his own version of frontier justice. Though what she hoped to accomplish by doing so, she didn't know. As tall as she was, every bit as tall as Lonnie, she was no match for the man and knew it. He was bullnecked, broad-shouldered and strong as an ox; even Duncan, half a head taller and in good shape himself, had always said he didn't have a prayer of beating Lonnie Doyle in a fair fight. Plus, the man was armed. And in a rage.

"What are you doing, man?" Al Hernandez, the other deputy, jerked at Lonnie's arm and half spun him around.

Lonnie shook off Al's hand. "What I shoulda done years ago. What I told Dunk he shoulda done. Shoulda drowned that cat the day he brought it home. I told him he was crazy. And lookit what's happened. Now I'm gonna kill that thing. I'm gonna shoot it right here and now!"

Al touched Lonnie's arm again. "Come on, man—"

"Not without a warrant, you're not." Brooke spoke loudly and calmly, and both men jerked their heads to look at her the way they might if the cougar itself had spoken. "This animal belongs to me," she went on, trying to keep her voice from quivering. "She is not an imminent threat to anybody now. You don't know what happened, or how it happened. You have no cause to shoot her, and if you try, you'll have to do it through me."

She saw Lonnie's small blue eyes glitter with a dangerous light, saw his jaw jut forward in a way she'd seen it do before, and wondered if she'd gone too far. She felt Daniel creep out from behind her to stand at her side. She felt his arm slip around her waist and wished, for his sake, she could stop shaking. She braced herself as Lonnie took a threatening step toward her.

But then Rosie came walking up, peeling off her gloves and shaking her head as she joined the two deputies. She spoke to them in a voice too low for Brooke to hear over the pounding in her head, and the two men turned and walked back to where the second EMT was packing up his gear. But not before Lonnie stabbed a finger at Brooke and said in a voice hoarse with fury, "This ain't over, Brooke. Count on it."

Rosie paused, looking uncertain, then came over to Brooke and reached out to lay a hand on her shoulder. "Brooke, Daniel—I'm so sorry. We did everything we could."

"I know you did. It's okay." Brooke felt her head nodding up and down, like a mechanical toy.

"Is there anything I can do? You want me to call Pastor Farley?"

"Yes, thank you. I'd appreciate that," Brooke murmured, although at that moment she didn't want to see or talk to anyone. All she wanted was to be alone with her son in her house, where she could fix him hot dogs for dinner and pretend the past thirty minutes or so hadn't happened. That it had all been a dream—a nightmare. She wanted desperately for it to all be a dream, a mistake, for there to be some sort of magic pill she could take to make it all go away.

Except she knew that wouldn't happen. And that the nightmare was just beginning.

Numbly, she watched the EMTs pack up their gear and make their way back through the barn to their parked vehicle. Al was speaking into the radio on his shoulder, calling for a forensics team, and Lonnie went loping off to the department SUV and returned carrying a roll of yellow plastic tape. Brooke had been the wife of a law enforcement officer for seven years; she knew what it all meant.

Her ex-husband, Daniel's father, was dead. This was a crime scene now.

Al finished talking into his radio and came over to where she and Daniel were standing, Daniel with his arm around her waist, still, his body rigid and straight as a post. Brooke, with her arm protectively around his shoulders, was the only one who'd know he was shaking, too. Al hauled in a breath and took on a cop's authoritative stance, with his thumbs hooked in his belt and his chest out.

"I'm gonna have to ask you to go on to the house now, if you wouldn't mind. We're gonna need to ask you some questions, but for right now, I need for you to move out of the way so we can do our job here, which is findin' out exactly what happened. You understand? We're gonna find out what happened to your husband."

*My ex-husband!* Brooke thought but only nodded.

Beside her, Daniel was shaking his head violently. "No—uh-uh, I'm not leaving. If we do, you'll shoot

Lady. And it wasn't her fault, what happened to Dad. I know it wasn't."

The deputy's stern cop face softened. He gave a little cough and said, "Now, son, nobody's gonna shoot your cat. I'm not gonna let that happen."

Daniel drew himself up and squared his shoulders. "You better promise." Brooke felt so proud, she almost smiled.

Al Hernandez did smile. "Yeah, son, I promise. There'll be an au—" he threw Brooke a look of apology, coughed again and said "—an investigation, and then a judge is gonna decide what to do about your cougar. Until that all happens, nobody's gonna touch her. Okay?"

Daniel didn't reply, and Brooke felt the resistance in his rigid body. The distrust. Though she understood just how he felt, she tightened her hold on his shoulders, and they left the compound together.

On the way to the house, she remembered the groceries still sitting in the truck. Daniel helped her carry them into the house and put them away, but when she asked him what he wanted for supper, he told her he wasn't hungry. Again, she knew how he felt but poured him a glass of orange juice, anyway, and as an afterthought, poured one for herself, too.

She pulled out a chair, and Daniel hitched himself sideways onto another, and they sat facing each other across the kitchen table, not looking directly at each other. Daniel took a cautious sip of his orange juice, then said, "I have homework."

Brooke took a sip of her juice and said, "What kind?"

"Math," said Daniel. "And social studies."

"I don't think you need to worry about that right now," Brooke told him, and he nodded and didn't ask why. That was the thing about Daniel; he understood so much without being told. Maybe too much for a child his age. Seen too much, too. Things no child of any age should have to see.

Brooke folded her hands together on the table in front of her and stared at them, marveling at how calm she felt. She wondered when it was going to hit her, the fact that Duncan was dead, killed by an animal she'd hand-raised from a kitten. And that he'd been found in a bloody mess by his nine-year-old son. She wondered when it was going to hit Daniel. She took a breath and looked at him and felt an awful twisting pain just below her heart.

"We have to talk," she said. "About what we're going to say when they ask us questions." Daniel continued to stare at his glass of orange juice. "Honey, I need you to tell me exactly what happened."

He drew a put-upon breath. "I already did. It was just like I said." He closed his eyes and went on in a singsong voice. "I got home, and I came in the house, and I got myself an ice-cream sandwich, and I heard Hilda barking, so I went out to see what was wrong, and I took the cell phone, because you told me I should always take it when I go out to the animals in case I need to call for help. And I saw…what I told you."

Forcing herself not to look at the fine blue veins in his eyelids or the bright spots of pink in his otherwise pale cheeks, Brooke persisted. "Honey, I'm sorry. They're going to ask you these things. Did you, um, look at your dad? Did you see any…" But she couldn't bring herself to ask him about the wounds. She didn't want to know about the wounds. Instead, choosing her words carefully, she said, "Daniel, did you see Lady bite your dad?"

He shook his head violently, and she saw him press his lips together hard for a moment before he answered, "No! I told you. She was just crouched down beside him, and she sort of…sniffed him, and then she pushed at him with her head—like this." He demonstrated. "Then she saw me, and she jumped back and started snarling and making that screaming noise and batting her paws at me. It was like—" He stopped, and the pink in his cheeks deepened.

"What, honey? It's okay. You can tell me."

He looked up at her at last, almost defiantly. "It was like she didn't want me to come in there, okay? Like she was trying to make me stay away. I know it sounds weird, but it was like she was trying to protect me. Like she didn't want me to see—"

"Oh, Daniel." Brooke wanted to smile at him, but the ache in her throat and in her whole face made it impossible. She could think of another reason for the cougar's behavior, of course, one more in keeping with the nature of a predator. She was probably trying to protect her "kill." *Sweetheart, don't you see that?*

But she didn't say it. So what if her son had found his own way of coping with the awfulness of what had happened? She'd let him keep whatever comfort he could for as long as he could.

"I knew you wouldn't believe me. That's why I didn't tell you," Daniel said as he scooted back his chair and carried his juice glass to the sink.

He was heading out of the kitchen, probably going to his room, but at that moment there was a knock on the kitchen door—the back door, the one they and nearly everyone who came to visit always used. Brooke could see Al Hernandez standing on the porch steps, looking off across the yard, where the CSI van and the medical examiner's wagon had joined the two sheriff's department SUVs. *Thank God,* she thought. That meant Lonnie would be out overseeing the processing of the crime scene and the…victim, and she was relieved not to have to deal with his anger and hostility. This was going to be difficult enough without that, she was sure.

When she went to let the deputy in, she saw that he had Hilda with him, on a makeshift rope leash. The dog was panting and grinning, interrupting herself frequently to lick her chops, a sure sign she was agitated. She'd been sitting quietly at Al's side, but when Brooke opened the screen door, she bounded past her, into the house, and Brooke could hear the scrabbling of toenails on the linoleum as she streaked across the kitchen, making, no doubt, for her favorite refuge, Daniel's room. She heard Daniel talking to the big dog in quiet tones as she nodded at the deputy and said, "Come on in, Al."

"Sorry about that," Al said, with a nod of his head in the general direction Hilda had taken. "I'd appreciate it if you could keep her in here until we're…uh, everything's done out here. She's been raising quite a ruckus."

"I can imagine," Brooke said, with a small huff of laughter—the nervous kind—and she wished she hadn't done it and made a note to herself not to do it again. She took a quick breath and added, "It's fine. I should have thought to bring her when I came in." She gestured toward the chair Daniel had been sitting in. "Have a seat. Can I get you anything?"

"No, ma'am. I am gonna need to talk to the boy, though. Is he—"

"I'm right here," Daniel said, coming into the kitchen. To Brooke, he said, "I put Hilda in my room, Mom. She's pretty upset."

"Daniel—" She held out her arm to bring him close, but he evaded her and instead pulled out another chair and sat down.

"I know. You want to ask me questions about what happened to my dad."

Brooke felt an unexpected urge to cry and clamped a hand over her mouth to stop it. Al Hernandez said, "That's right, son. I need you to tell me everything you can about what happened out there. Can you do that?"

Daniel said, "Sure," and went on to tell his story again, without the smarty-pants tone he'd used with Brooke, while Al jotted notes in a notebook he'd taken out of his uniform pocket.

"So, that's the first you knew anything was wrong?" Al asked when he'd finished. "When you heard the dog barking?" Daniel nodded. "And you didn't see anybody around the place? Hear anybody? Any cars?" Daniel shook his head. "And your dad—he didn't come here, to the house?"

Daniel shook his head again, rapidly this time, and began to fidget in his chair. "No, I didn't see him. I haven't seen him for a while, actually. Next weekend's his weekend to have me. I don't usually see him otherwise." His face was very pale, so that the freckles across his nose and the tops of his cheeks stood out like sprinkles of sand.

Al must have noticed it, too, because his eyes and voice were kind as he said, "Okay, son, that's fine. I think that's all. You did fine."

"So," said Daniel, "can I go now?"

"Sure, go on. Take care of your dog." The deputy waited until Daniel had disappeared down the hall and they heard the thump of the closing door. Then he leveled a look that was considerably less kind at Brooke and said, "Okay, now I'll ask you the same thing. Tell me exactly what you saw and did. Your son said you were gone when this happened?"

She cleared her throat and nodded. "Yes, that's right. I'd gone to town for feed and groceries, and I was late getting back because—" she gave that nervous laugh she'd promised herself she wouldn't "—well, I guess you don't want to know all that."

Al just looked at her and waited for her to go on. She told herself she had no reason to be nervous, but she was. So nervous her mouth felt like dust. She clasped her hands together in front of her on the tabletop and tried to make them look relaxed. Natural.

"Um…anyway, when I got home, the first thing I saw was Duncan's SUV parked on that back road, the one that goes around the property. I thought—" She paused, but Al just nodded and didn't interrupt. "I thought it was strange, him being there, but I came on to the house, and then I thought it was strange that Hilda—that's the dog—and Daniel didn't come running out to meet me, like they usually do. It wasn't until I turned off the motor and was getting out of the truck that I heard the noise."

"What did you hear, exactly?"

"I heard Hilda barking, and then I heard Lady—the cougar—scream. And that's when I ran." Her voice had begun to shake. She fought to control it while the deputy waited patiently, staring down at the notes he'd made.

She wished she could get up and get a glass of water. She wished she could run to her bedroom and crawl under the covers and pull a pillow over her head.

After a moment, she drew a quivering breath and went on. She described everything that had happened, and when she was finished, she was surprised to discover she'd been crying. For some reason, that embarrassed her, and she tried to wipe the tears away surreptitiously while Al was still looking down, writing in his notebook. She waited for him to ask more questions, and when he didn't, she cleared her throat again and said, "Al, can I ask you something?"

He glanced up, frowning.

"What did he—I mean, how did he look? You know, were the wounds…" She touched her lips with her fingertips, and more tears rolled down her cheeks. This time she didn't try to wipe them away. "I just really need to know. Did Lady kill him?"

"Ma'am, I can't make that kind of judgment. That's up to the ME." He paused, then seemed to relent. "I will tell you there's some blood on Dunk's clothes, and some—not a lot—on the ground. We'll just have to wait for the autopsy to determine how he died. Now, if you don't mind, I have just a few more questions…"

He asked her about the compound, the gate, how it was locked up and who had a key. He asked her how she thought Duncan might have gotten into the pen with the cougar, and why.

"That's what I can't imagine," Brooke said in a whisper. "Duncan was deathly afraid of that cat, although he'd never have admitted it. He always wanted to get rid of it. When I told him I wanted to start a refuge for big cats—you know, like, animals people take as pets, then can't take care of when they get big and dangerous—he thought I was nuts. He even insisted on buying a tranquilizer gun, just in case, because he said he knew I'd never be able to shoot her, if it came to that." Her voice broke, and as she paused to control it, a thought occurred to her. "I wonder why he didn't— Duncan, I mean. Didn't he have his gun?"

Al gave her an unreadable look. "It wasn't on him, no, ma'am. We found it in his vehicle."

He tucked his notebook and pencil back in his pocket and rose. "I guess that's all—for now. We'll be in touch once the medical examiner's done." He thanked her, nodded a farewell and left the way he'd come, through the back door.

Brooke sat where he'd left her, with one hand covering her mouth and her eyes closed, listening to the sounds of vehicles coming and going outside in the yard, and the distant mutter of men's voices. She didn't want to listen to the voices rumbling around inside her own head, but they kept intruding, anyway.

*Something isn't right about this. I can feel it. Something's not right. It doesn't make sense.*

Either Daniel wasn't telling her the whole story, or…or what? She didn't know. Only that something was wrong.

After a while—she didn't know how long—she realized the noises outside had stopped. That all the official vehicles had gone. Finally. The sun had gone down. It was past time to feed the animals. Only her ingrained sense of responsibility made her get up and go outside and throw some hay to the two horses, six goats and two alpacas, and close and bar the chicken-house door. She didn't go down to the far end of the corrals, where Lady's compound was. The cougar was in her holding cage and would be all right where she was until tomorrow.

Back in the house, she went to check on Daniel and Hilda and found both in Daniel's bed, sound asleep on top of the covers. Daniel had one arm thrown across the dog's body, and Hilda had her muzzle resting on the boy's chest. She went to her own room and got a comforter and spread it over the softly snoring pair. Then, after a moment, she lifted the edge of the comforter and lay down, stretching herself out beside her son. With her arm across his body and her face nestled in his damp hair, breathing the salty, small-boy smell of him, she fell asleep.

In the morning, she was in the kitchen, making blueberry pancakes—Daniel's favorite breakfast—when the knock came. Not on the kitchen door, the one everyone always used, but on the front door. Her hands shook slightly as she wiped them on a dish towel and went down the hall and through the living room to answer it.

Sheriff Clayton Carter stood on her front porch. He was wearing his brown Stetson, and his arms were folded across the front of his unbuttoned Western-style jacket. He didn't smile or remove his hat when Brooke opened the door, and she didn't smile and say that it was a nice surprise to see him and ask if he would care to come in for coffee.

"Ma'am, would you step out here please?" the sheriff said.

Moving as if in a dream, Brooke did, and two uniformed deputies she didn't know came up the steps behind the sheriff, and one of them took her arm and turned her around.

"Brooke Fallon Grant," the sheriff said, "I'm placing you under arrest for the murder of Duncan Grant. You have the right to remain silent...."

Then Brooke's head filled with the sound of high winds, and for some time she didn't hear anything else. Not until she was in the sheriff's car and being driven out of the yard, and she looked back and saw Daniel being restrained by one of the uniformed deputies. She heard his shrill and stricken cry.

"Mom! *Mama*..."

# Chapter 2

The last thing Holt Kincaid had expected to encounter when he drove into Colton, Texas, was a traffic jam. According to the information he'd gotten off the Internet, the population still hadn't topped seven thousand, probably due to the fact that the town was just outside reasonable commuting distance from both Austin and San Antonio, and its residents hadn't yet figured out how to capitalize on its Hill Country charm and local history to bring in the tourist trade. From what Holt could see, the town's two main industries appeared to be peaches and rocks, and while there was still an apparently endless supply of the latter—in spite of the fact that nearly all the buildings on the main drag were constructed out of them—the season for the former was pretty much over. And it didn't seem likely the excess of vehicular traffic was due to rush hour, either, since it was mid-morning and, anyway, in his experience in towns like this, what passed for "rush hour" usually coincided with the start and end of the school day.

Also, it didn't seem likely that local traffic, no matter how heavy, could account for the high number of vans and panel trucks he was seeing, with satellite antennas sprouting out of their tops and news-station logos painted on their sides.

During his slow progress through the center of town, Holt was able to discern that the excitement seemed to be centered around the elaborate and somewhat over-sized Gothic-style, stone—of course—courthouse, which was located a block off the highway, down the main cross street. A crowd had gathered on the grassy square in front of the courthouse, everyone sort of milling around in the shade of several big oak trees, the way people do when they're bored to death but expecting something exciting to happen any minute.

The sense of anticipation—almost euphoria—with which he'd entered the town, certain he was almost at the end of what had been a long and often frustrating quest, was replaced now by a sense of caution, developed over his long years of experience as a private investigator with a specialty in finding people. While it didn't seem likely this unexpected gathering of news media could have anything to do with his reason for being here in the town of Colton, he figured it wouldn't hurt to know exactly what he was getting into the middle of.

A few blocks past the courthouse, the traffic thinned out considerably, and Holt pulled off onto a side street and found a parking spot across from a diner, the inauspicious kind frequented by locals rather than passing-through motorists looking for a familiar franchise.

On his way into the diner, he dropped a quarter into a box dispensing the local newspaper, which he folded in half and tucked under his arm as he made his way past empty booths to take a seat at the counter—also empty, except for a waitress taking her mid-morning coffee break. Holt had an idea the usual denizens of the place could probably be found among the crowd down at the courthouse.

As he was taking his seat on one of the cracked red vinyl and chrome stools, the waitress wiped her mouth with a paper napkin, slid off her stool and swept, with a flourish, around the end of the counter to present herself behind the section he'd just occupied.

"Hi," she chirped. "My name is Shirley, and I'll be your server today. How may I help you?" And then she gave a throaty chortle to show she was just putting him on, and said in what Holt imagined was her natural Texas twang, "What can I get for ya, hon?"

Shirley was a heavyset woman in her forties, probably, with Day-Glo red curls piled on top of her head and laugh lines radiating from the corners of her vivid blue eyes. She had a nice smile, so Holt smiled back and said, "Coffee, for starters." He tilted his head toward the glass case behind the counter. "And maybe a piece of that pie there. Is that peach?"

"Sure is," Shirley said, beaming. "Local, too. And the season's 'bout over, so you hit it just right. Can I put a scoop of ice cream on that for ya?"

"No thanks—got to watch my waistline." He patted himself in that general area, and Shirley gave him a severe look and what could only be described as a snort.

"Oh, sure, like you need to worry. Mister, you turn sideways, you'd just 'bout disappear." While she was saying this, she was efficiently dishing up a slice of pie and placing it in front of him, with a fork and a spoon beside it.

Holt waited until a mug of steaming coffee had joined the pie, then picked up the fork and said, "Where is everybody?"

Shirley made that same inelegant noise as she leaned against the stainless-steel counter behind her and folded her arms across her ample bosom. "Down at the courthouse, probably. Along with just about ever'body else in this town. It's where I'd be, too, if I wasn't stuck holdin' down the fort here."

Holt dug into the pie, which was delicious, maybe the best fresh peach pie he'd ever eaten. "I saw the media trucks as I was coming through. What's all the excitement about?"

Shirley tipped her head toward his left arm. "Well, you could read all about it in that paper you got propping up your elbow there. One of our local deputy sheriffs got killed a couple days ago—by a mountain lion, it looked like. And then they went and arrested his wife— ex-wife, I should say—for murder. Biggest thing to happen around here in a while, I'll tell you. The whole state of Texas seems to have caught it now, too— because it was a cop that got killed, I guess. Or the lion angle, maybe. Anyway, it sure is a shame. They had a kid, too, a little boy. I guess he's been staying with the preacher at their church."

Holt didn't hear anything more. While the waitress had been talking, he'd unfolded the newspaper and spread it out next to his pie plate. There was the headline, pretty much the way she'd summed it up: Local Deputy Killed By Lion, Ex-wife Arrested, and under that a was photo of the deputy in his dress uniform, complete with Stetson. Holt had started skimming the article and had got as far as the name of the woman who'd been arrested and charged with murdering her ex-husband, Duncan Grant. The name jumped out at him, and it was about like having a rattlesnake coil up and strike right at his chest. *Brooke Fallon Grant.* Shirley's voice faded into a soft roar, and hot coffee slopped out of the mug and burned his hand.

"Oh—my goodness. Here let me…" Shirley was there with a towel, mopping up. "Hope ya didn't burn yourself. Coffee's pretty hot. Just made a fresh pot…"

He frowned distractedly at her, then relinquished the coffee mug, and she whisked it away and brought him a new one while he tried to absorb the words printed on the newspaper page in front of him.

*Mrs. Grant was arrested at her home Thursday morning after an autopsy revealed the presence of large amounts of a tranquilizer in the victim's body. According to sources at the medical examiner's office, the drug had evidently been administered by a tranquilizer dart gun, the type used to subdue large animals.*

*Deputy Grant's body was discovered by his young son Wednesday afternoon in an animal enclosure on his ex-wife's ranch. The enclosure had been used to house a mountain lion allegedly hand-raised by Mrs. Grant. The animal was found in close proximity to Deputy Grant's body and was assumed to have killed him. However, in light of the new evidence revealed by the autopsy, it is not clear now what part the animal might have played in the deputy's death.*

*According to information received by this reporter, Mr. and Mrs. Grant had recently been involved in a dispute over custody of the couple's nine-year-old son.*

*Arraignment and bail hearing are set to take place Friday afternoon at the courthouse in Colton. A hearing to determine the fate of the mountain lion has not been scheduled, pending further investigation. As the county lacks facilities to house the animal, the mountain lion remains in its compound on Mrs. Grant's ranch.*

*In the absence of any known relatives, the couple's son is being cared for by the pastor of Mrs. Grant's church pending the outcome of Friday's hearing.*

"Yeah, it sure is a shame." Shirley was shaking her head. "I used to see Duncan in here now and again. All the deputies like to come in for the pie, you know. I didn't know him all that well, though—I was a few years ahead of him in school. Never met his wife… I don't know, though…seems like a pretty heartless thing to do, doesn't it? I mean, raise a cougar from a cub— or whatever you call a baby one—and then try and blame it for killing somebody? And letting your little boy find his daddy's body? Hard to imagine a mother doing something like that."

"Sounds like the paper's got her pretty much tried and convicted," Holt said dryly as he slid off the stool and reached for his wallet.

Shirley made that sound again. "Yeah, well, this is kind of a small town, and the local law is real…visible, if you know what I mean. So…you're not plannin' on stayin' around to see how it comes out?"

"Actually, I might stay around for a bit." He laid some bills down on the counter and picked up the paper and tucked it under his arm. "S'pose you could recommend a nice, quiet motel for me? Or have all these media people got everything booked?"

"Seriously." She gave him a wry smile as she scooped up the bills with one hand and the dishes with the other. "They've been pouring into town all day. I'd say you'd probably have to go a ways to find a room."

"Yeah, I figured. Thanks, anyway. Great coffee, by the way. And the best peach pie I ever ate." Holt gave her his nicest smile and turned to go.

"Wait."

With one hand on the door, Holt turned. Shirley was gazing at him in a speculative way and chewing her lip.

"Okay, look, I don't know why, but you strike me as a nice guy. There's a motel just west of here, just off the main drag. It's called the Cactus Country Inn—it's not a chain or a Best Western, or anything, but it's nice. My brother and his wife manage it. They usually keep the room next to their apartment empty, on account of the walls are kinda thin, if you know what I mean. But if you tell 'em I sent you, they'll probably let you have it. Just don't throw any wild parties, though, okay?"

"I think I can promise that," Holt said.

An hour or so later, he sat on the edge of one of two neatly made-up twin-size beds in a fairly decent room—he couldn't remember if he'd ever been in a motel room that had twin-size beds before—in the Cactus Country Inn. He punched a number on his cell phone speed dial and while he listened to it ring, imagined it ringing in a room far away, in South Carolina, on the shores of a small lake. It rang four times before a machine picked up.

"Hello. You've reached Sam and Cory's place. We're both away from home right now. Leave us a message, and we'll get back to you…."

He disconnected and sat for a moment with the phone in his hand, thinking. Then he pulled the laptop that lay open on the bed closer to him, found the page he was looking for, scrolled down the list of phone numbers on it until he came to the one he wanted. Dialed it.

Several minutes and several different numbers later, he'd learned several things. One, his employer was on assignment in the Sudan, and there was no way in hell to reach him. Two, his employer's wife was also on assignment; only God—and the CIA—knew where.

Three, he was on his own.

Holt Kincaid didn't often feel frustrated, but he did now. Here he'd finally managed to get a line on one of his client's missing twin sisters, and there wasn't anybody he could break the news to.

News that wasn't good.

And he was very much afraid that if he waited for the clients to return from their various assignments, it might be too late. So, he hesitated for another second, maybe, then scrolled on down to the bottom of the list of phone numbers on his computer screen, to the first one listed under the heading In Case of Emergency. He was pretty sure Sam and Cory would agree that finding the subject of their years-long search about to be locked up for murder would qualify as an emergency.

He punched the number into his cell phone and hit the call button.

Tony Whitehall was sitting on his mother's patio, watching his numerous nieces and nephews engaged in mayhem disguised as a game of touch football. The game was probably more fraught with violence than it might have been, due to the fact that it was being played on hard bare dirt, since his mother, being more than half Apache and a native not only of America but the great desert Southwest, had better sense than to try to get a lawn to grow on it. His mother did like flowers, though, which she grew in pots near her front doorsteps, where she could water them with a plastic gallon jug. The rest of her land-scaping consisted mostly of native plants—junipers and ocotillos and barrel cactus and tamarisks for windbreaks and some stubborn cottonwoods and willows along the creek bed, where for two months or so in the spring a trickle of water actually flowed.

For shade, there was the colorful striped fabric of the umbrellas and awnings, which mostly covered the patio that Tony was enjoying, along with a cold beer, when his cell phone rang. That surprised him, first, because cell phone service out here in the wilds of Arizona wasn't all that reliable, and second, because most of the people who had his private cell number were already here.

He fumbled around and managed to get the phone out of his pocket and opened up and the right button pushed before the thing went to voice mail. "Yeah," he said, then remembered to add, "Uh…Tony Whitehall."

Then he had to stick a finger in his ear to hear the person on the other end, because a gaggle of his sisters were at that moment gathered around their mother on the other side of the patio and were exhorting her loudly and passionately about losing some weight. This was an argument they were bound to lose, since Rosetta White-hall was quite content with herself just as she was and was countering her daughters' concerns as she always did by pointing out certain facts: "The women in my family have always been big, and we've always been happy, and we make our men happy, too!"

At the moment, Tony was just happy to have his sisters' attention focused for a few minutes on something else besides him and his persistent state of bachelorhood. The poking and prying and teasing and nagging was something he'd been putting up with since he'd reached the age of puberty, but lately it had begun to grate on his nerves.

The voice in his ear was still an unintelligible mumble, so he said, "Hold on, I can't hear you," and got up and walked across the patio and made his way around the corner of the house, where he'd be out of vocal range of both the football game and the sisters. "Yeah…okay. So who did you say this is?"

"Sorry. My name is Holt Kincaid. I'm a private investigator. I'm working for a friend of yours—Cory Pearson—tracking down his brothers and sisters, who got separated from him when he was a kid."

"Oh yeah…yeah, I knew about that. Found his brothers already, I heard. Fantastic. That's great. So why are you—"

"Cory gave me your name and number, told me to call you if anything came up while he was on assignment and I couldn't reach either him or Sam—his wife. So…they're both on assignment, and…something's come up. So, I'm calling."

"Wow. So…what? You find the baby sisters?"

"Well, yeah, one of them, but—"

"Hey, no kidding? That's *great*, man!"

"Yeah, well, maybe not. There's…a problem."

"Oh, yeah? What kind of problem?"

"It's a little complicated to explain over the phone, and this is a terrible connection, anyway. How fast can you get to Colton, Texas?"

Gazing off across the dirt yard to where the football game was still in noisy progress, Tony could hear that the voices of his sisters around the corner on the patio had died to a frustrated mutter. Which meant they'd be turning their attention back to him the minute he showed his face again.

"Colton—whereabouts in Texas is that?"

"Uh…roughly southwest of Austin and northeast of nowhere. Hill Country."

"Okay, how's about tonight? Say around dinnertime."

"What? Where in hell are you?"

"At the moment I'm in Arizona, at my mom's. It's her birthday. Talk about northeast of nowhere. Otherwise I'd be there sooner."

"Are you crazy? That's gotta be eight or nine hundred miles."

"What? You think I'm gonna drive it? Across West Texas? Now, that would be crazy. Hey, do me a favor, okay? Check and see if this town you're in has a general-aviation airfield. Failing that, any kind of level airstrip… piece of road—hell, even a cow pasture without too many rocks."

"I can tell you right now, *that's* not gonna happen," the voice on the other end of the phone said dryly. "But I'll look into the airfield and get back to you."

"Cool. I'm on my way."

Tony disconnected the phone and stuck it back in his pocket, then took a breath and summoned the courage to go and break the news to his mother that he was going to be leaving her birthday party a little sooner than expected.

Brooke's lawyer was an old-school Texan, a grandfatherly sort named Sam Houston Henderson, from her father's old law firm in Austin. He drove her home after the bail hearing and left her surrounded by a welcoming committee consisting of Daniel; Pastor Steven Farley and his wife, Myra; Rocky and Isabel Miranda, her neighbors from across the road who'd been looking after the animals in her absence; and of course, Hilda, who almost knocked them all flat in her exuberant joy at having the missing members of her "flock" all together and back under her protection again. Brooke was glad to be back, too, of course, but her relief was tempered by what the lawyer had told her in the car on the way home.

"Now, Brooke, honey, you know just because the judge granted you bail doesn't mean you're out of the woods on this thing. You got bail because you've got sole responsibility for your boy and your animals, and because pretty much everything you own is tied up in your place and in that trust your daddy set up for you. So it's not likely you'd be goin' anywhere. And it's also not likely you'd be a further danger to society, so there just wasn't any justification in keepin' you locked up. But that is a deputy sheriff and a local boy you're accused of killin', so we've got one hell of an uphill fight ahead of us. You know that, don't you?"

"What about Lady?" Brooke had asked.

"Lady—oh, yeah, the cougar. Well, now…"

"Lonnie Doyle is going to do his best to have her put down."

"I'm gonna be honest with you, Brooke. It's gonna be tough to argue that lion isn't a dangerous animal. She did maul your husband—"

"Ex-husband."

"—and she did draw blood, whether that was what killed him or not. But for now I don't want you to worry about that. We've got some time before they get around to a hearing about the cat, and right now you need to get yourself rested up so we can figure out how to fight this battle we're in. Okay? Now, you go on and enjoy being with your boy, and have a quiet weekend, and I'll talk to you next week."

"Yes, sir," Brooke had murmured, and now she stood safe in her own home, surrounded by the warmth and love of her son, her dog and her good friends the Farleys and the Mirandas.

"It's gonna be okay, Mom," Daniel whispered as he let her hug him longer than usual.

"I know. Of course, it is." But as she watched Sam Houston Henderson's taillights turn the corner at the end of the lane, inside she felt nothing but cold and hollow and scared to death.

"Must be nice, having your own plane," Holt said to his passenger as they sped back to town on the two-lane FM road that connected it to its surprisingly busy airfield. He'd discovered airfields of the kind that served the town of Colton were pretty common in Texas, which made sense, seeing as how airplanes were probably the most practical means of bridging the enormous distances between anyplace and anyplace else in that part of the country.

"Yeah," Tony said, "the kinds of places my job takes me, sometimes it's about the only way to get there." He looked over at Holt. "Matter of fact, it was your client's wife—Sam—she's the one that taught me to fly."

"That right?"

"We had an…adventure, the three of us, a few years back. In the Philippines. Kind of got me hooked on vintage planes, I guess. She was flying a World War II Gooney Bird at the time. Mine's a little later vintage than that, though—1979 Piper Cherokee. I've got her equipped for long-range flying—extra fuel tanks and all that. Places I go, refueling can be a problem."

Holt glanced at the man taking up what seemed like more than his share of space in the car. From what little chance he'd had to take the man's measure, Holt couldn't in any way, shape or form call him overweight, so it must be something to do with charisma, he decided, that made Tony Whitehall seem larger than life. "So, you're a photographer?"

"Photojournalist," Tony corrected, but with a forgiving grin.

That was another thing Holt had noticed right away, the easygoing but straightforward manner that made a person both like and trust the man instinctively. He was beginning to see why Cory Pearson had put him at the top of his list of people to go to in an emergency.

"Well, you're gonna fit right in, in Colton," he said dryly. "The place is a zoo. Crawling with news media."

"Yeah?" Tony shifted around to look at him. "This wouldn't have anything to do with the 'problem' you mentioned, would it?"

"It would." Holt stared at the road ahead and thought about where to begin. Finally, he said, "You said you knew we found the boys, right? Cory's two brothers. Last summer. Found Wade—the oldest—first. He was a cop up in Portland. And since the two boys had been adopted by the same couple, he put us right in touch with Matt, down in LA."

"Right, and now you say you found the girls?" Tony prompted, but not in an impatient way.

"*One* of the girls." Holt let out a breath. "I thought it was gonna be a cakewalk once I found out they'd been adopted together, too. But turns out the parents were both killed a couple of years ago in a car wreck, along with their biological son—he was quite a bit older than the twins. I found out that this one—Brooke—had married and moved here to Colton. Married a cop, actually. Deputy sheriff. But there wasn't a thing about the other twin—Brenna. Nothing from high school on. She just disappears at that point. So, anyway, I come here to Colton to get a line on Brooke. Scope out the lay of the land, you know? Like I did when I found Wade. Wanted to see how things were, get an idea who this person was before I went to Cory with it. So we'd know the best way to spring the news, you know?"

"I hear you," Tony said, nodding. "You don't just walk up to a stranger and say, 'Hi, there. I'm the brother you didn't know you had.'"

"Right. And it's an even safer bet the twins wouldn't have any idea about having three older brothers, since they were practically just babies when they all got separated. So anyway, I get to Colton, and I find the town in an uproar because one of their deputy sheriffs has just been killed. Originally, it was supposed to have been a mountain lion that killed him—"

"Oh, wow—I saw something about that. It was on CNN just the other night. The cougar was the guy's ex-wife's pet, right? And their little boy found his dad's body. Supposedly an accident, I thought. I didn't get a chance to see the news today—it was my mom's birthday, and the festivities started pretty early. So now—oh, man, don't tell me. *This* is the missing twin? The dead guy's wife?"

"Ex-wife. And it's not an accident anymore. Seems they found something in the autopsy that puts a whole new light on things. In any event, they've arrested my client's baby sister for murder. First degree, premeditated. And in Texas, don't forget, they still have the death penalty. And use it."

Tony uttered a word his mother wouldn't have approved of.

"My sentiments exactly," Holt said.

"So what's the plan?" Tony asked Holt over a club sandwich at a local diner not far from the Cactus Country Inn, where they were staying. A club sandwich was pretty much Tony's standard order when he was in an unfamiliar eatery, since it was pretty hard to ruin one, but watching Holt chomp into his big, thick, juicy burger, he was beginning to regret his choice. "Somehow I don't think me being a photographer is going to get me an in with this lady just now."

The PI nodded as he chewed, then swallowed and said, "Yeah, I know. We're going to have to come up with something—" He broke off, and Tony watched him in amusement as he coughed and tried not to make it too obvious what he was thinking. Something along the lines of, *This guy looks like a bouncer in a mob hangout, and I'm supposed to get him close to a woman who right now is not likely to be trusting anybody short of Dr. Phil?* But it didn't bother him. He was used to it.

"How 'bout the lion?" he said, taking pity on the guy. "I can make it about the cat."

Holt raised his eyebrows over his burger as he prepared to take another bite. "Hmm. Maybe."

"No, seriously. I've done some wildlife pieces before. The reintroduction of wolves into Yellowstone, poaching elephant ivory…stuff like that. Plus—" he grinned around the sandwich he was biting into "—I have a thing for mountain lions."

Holt's eyes narrowed. "A…*thing*."

Tony thought, *Me and my big mouth.* He didn't know what it was that had made him mention to this stranger something so personal he hadn't even told his best friends, Cory and Sam, about it. But it had been the reason the CNN piece had caught his attention in the first place— the bit about the lion. Now he had to find some way to explain without giving up more personal information than he wanted to. "It's an Indian thing. It's my spirit animal. Or so my mama says." He gave a self-deprecating half shrug.

"No kidding? 'My brother, the lion'—that kind of thing?"

"A little more than that. Hey, it's complicated, and to tell you the truth, I'm not sure my mama's people— they're Apache—were totally into that, anyway. I think she just told me that spirit messenger stuff when I was a little kid to make me get over being scared."

"Of the bogeyman, you mean."

"Something like that." And that was as far as Tony was willing to go on the subject. "Anyway, let's just say

I can make a pretty good case for why she ought to let me do a piece on her cougar."

"Sounds good to me," Holt said as he polished off the last bite of his burger and reached for his coffee. "Let's hope it's good enough."

## Chapter 3

Tony hadn't expected to be welcomed by Brooke Fallon Grant, accused murderer, with open arms. On the other hand, he hadn't exactly been prepared to find a shaggy tan-and-white dog the approximate size of a Shetland pony and a little blond kid armed with a rake— a *rake?*—blocking the driveway to her house.

He halted the rented sedan he'd borrowed from Holt in the middle of the tree-shaded lane and ran the window down. He stuck his head out, smiled winningly and called, "Hey, there. I'm looking for Brooke Grant. Would that be your mom?"

"Maybe." The boy was holding the rake with both hands, crossways in front of him, not smiling back. "But she's not here."

Tony got out of the car and stood with one elbow leaning on the top of the open door. The kid took a step backward, then held his ground. The dog looked alert but wasn't growling, which Tony took as a positive sign. "Well, now," he said, still smiling, "I see there's a pickup truck parked up there by the house, and you look pretty young to be the driver. Are you sure your mom's not home?"

"Okay, she is, but she doesn't want to see anybody." The boy let go of the rake with one hand and reached into the pocket of his jeans. "If you don't leave, I'm calling nine-one-one on my cell. I have it right here, see?" He produced the object and pointed it at Tony like a pistol.

Tony put his hands in the air. "Hey, okay, son. I'm not here to bother anybody. Look, is it okay if I give you my card?" Not waiting for an answer, which he was pretty sure he wouldn't like, he took out the card he'd put in his shirt pocket for just such an eventuality. He showed it to the kid, then leaned over the open door and placed it on the hood of the car.

Looking as menacing as it's possible for a skinny kid with silky blond hair to look, the boy sidled close enough to snatch up the card, then retreated to his comfort zone and gave it a good look. "It says here you're a photojournalist." He gave Tony a sideways look of suspicion and hostility. "That's like a reporter, right? My mom for *sure* doesn't want to talk to any reporters." He began to thumb the cell phone.

Tony said, "No—wait," and stepped around the door. The dog advanced a step, tail held low and not wagging. Tony hastily returned to his previous position behind the door. "Um, see…it's *like* a reporter, yeah, but I'm not here about your mom, or your…uh, anything like that. Look, what I'm interested in, actually, is your lion."

"Lady?" The boy looked surprised, then uncertain and, consequently, very young. And when he lifted his chin, the combination of vulnerability and defiance made something quiver in the general vicinity of Tony's heart. "She didn't do what they said she did. But they want to put her down, anyway."

"Who does?"

"The sheriffs. Lonnie Doyle, mostly—he's my dad's partner. He says Lady's a killer and she should be put down. But she didn't hurt Dad, at least not on purpose. I know she didn't."

"Well, then," Tony said gently, "sounds like all the more reason to get her story out there, doesn't it? Look here—my Web site address is on that card. Why don't you go ask your mom if you can look me up on the Internet? I'll wait right here while you do it. How's that?"

The boy chewed his lip for a moment; then up came the chin again. "Okay, but you better not come any closer. Hilda, *watch him*," he said to the dog, then turned and headed back up the lane at a dead run.

The dog flopped down on her stomach with her paws in front of her in the attitude of the Sphinx and fixed him with her unblinking stare.

"Good dog," said Tony hopefully and settled down to wait.

"Mom, I think you should talk to him."

"Honey, he's a *photographer*."

"Uh-uh. A *photojournalist*."

"That means he's a reporter. Even worse."

"Uh-uh, I don't think so. He's won awards. It says so right there. And anyway, it's not you he wants to do a story about. It's Lady."

"Of course he'd *say* that. Honey, it's probably just a ploy."

"What's a *ploy*?"

"An angle—a gimmick. A way to get to us. Daniel—"

"I don't think so, Mom." He hitched himself halfway onto a chair and faced her across the kitchen table, his face flushed and earnest. "I don't know why, but I don't think he's lying. He's…I don't know how to explain it—"

"He *looks* nice, is that it?" *Oh, sweetheart, if only it were that easy to tell.*

Her son's expression was impossible to describe. "No. He doesn't. That's what's so weird. He looks really tough and mean, but—" He huffed in a breath, leaned his chin on one hand and pressed his lips together in concentration. Then he said, "It's like…in the movies when there's somebody that always plays the bad guy, and then suddenly he's in a movie, and he's the *good* guy for a change. And he still *looks* like the bad guy, but you just know he's not. Like when Arnold Swarzenegger was really bad in *The Terminator*, but then he was really really good in *Terminator 2*. Like that."

Brooke hesitated, running her thumb over the smooth surface of the small brown card in her hand. What if it was true? What if this man—Daniel's "good guy" Terminator—could help save Lady's life? *And maybe mine, too?*

Daniel slid off the chair with a long-suffering sigh. "Well, can we at *least* check him out on the Internet?"

Brooke gave an exhalation of her own and capitulated. "Sure," she said, handing him the card. "Why not?"

"Your card neglected to mention that one of those awards was a Pulitzer."

Tony jerked out of a heat-and-boredom-induced doze, closed his mouth and focused on the woman standing on the other side of the open car door. His first thought was, *Wow.* His second, more coherent, thought was, *Okay, tall, slim and blond—I see where the kid gets it.* His third thought, as he scrubbed a hand over his face and struggled to extricate himself from the driver's seat, was *Oh man, I hope I wasn't snoring.*

Being as how Brooke Fallon Grant was his buddy Cory's sister and his buddy Cory was a pretty good-looking guy, he hadn't been expecting a troll. But the woman standing before him with her fingertips poked into the back pockets of her jeans, regarding him with a not-at-all-sure-I-should-be-doing-this look on her face…well, the only word that suited her was *lovely.*

Tony had a photographer's eye, of course, one that saw beyond the fatigue lines, no makeup, and hair that was limp and dull and in need of washing. What he saw was dark blue eyes like Cory's, eyes that told you they'd seen more than they wanted to of the world's sadness and suffering. And amazing bones, the kind that made him itch to reach for his camera. Which was too bad, because he was pretty sure the first time he aimed a lens in the lady's direction, she'd sic that monster dog on him.

*At the very least.* He'd forgotten for a moment that he might be looking at the face of a cold-blooded killer.

Though strangely, all his instincts were screaming, *No way!*

"Tony Whitehall," he said, holding out his hand and turning on every watt of charm he had in him. "Mrs. Grant, thanks for seeing me."

"Thank my son, Daniel." She offered him half a smile along with her hand, which was big-boned for a woman's hand and strong. "He's convinced you're a good guy."

*But you're not, are you?* "Really?" he said. "Wow, coulda fooled me." His eyes dropped—though not far—to the dog, now standing relaxed beside her mistress and panting lazily. "That's quite a pair of watchdogs you've got."

She glanced down as her hand came to rest on the dog's broad white head, and the camera shutter in Tony's mind clicked madly. "They're very protective of me. Both of them are."

*I see what Daniel means,* Brooke thought.

There was just something about the man. Something that had nothing to do with his looks, certainly, because he couldn't by any means be called handsome or even nice-looking. He had a hawkish nose and broad cheekbones and dark, mahogany-toned skin, but under it his face seemed to almost glow with a kind of inner warmth. The warmth was there, too, in his hazel eyes, which were odd—shocking, even—in such a dark face. And in his smile, which was wide and generous and revealed an intriguing dimple in one cheek. He was completely bald—she thought he probably shaved his head—

which, coupled with his powerful shoulders and chest, ought to have made him look like a thug but somehow only enhanced an indefinable but undeniable *presence*. He wasn't tall—probably only a little taller than she was—but he seemed larger-than-life, and, at the same time, rock-solid, down-to-earth, completely human.

What the man had, she realized, was charisma. Oodles of it. Not to mention charm, of course, with those eyes and that smile.

"That's good," he was saying. "Understandable."

*Oh, yeah—and a voice that sounds the way fur feels...*

She drew her defenses around herself and said, with stiff politeness, "So, Daniel tells me you're interested in our Lady."

The smile splashed warmth across his face. "Lady— that's her name? Your cougar?"

"Daniel named her. She had a brother named Tramp, but he died just two days after we got them."

"How *did* you come by a pair of cougar kittens, or lion cubs, or whatever they're called?" His eyes seemed to glow with interest.

Staring into them, she realized she'd moved without consciousness, gravitated closer to where he stood in the open doorway of his car. Whoever he was, she thought as she took two quick steps backward, good guy or bad, in his own way Tony Whitehall was dangerous.

She said sharply, "I haven't decided whether I want to tell you that yet. But if we're going to discuss it, you should probably come up to the house. It's too hot to stand here in the road."

She turned and walked away, back up the lane, and

behind her she heard him say, "Yeah—okay. Sure." And then the car door closed and the engine fired. A moment later, the sedan came prowling slowly past her.

She gave him points for having the good sense not to stop and offer her a ride.

The house was stone, like most Tony'd seen in the Hill Country so far—the older ones, anyway. It sat on a little rise and had a wide front porch that looked out toward the lane and the live oaks and the paved road below. But the real view, he saw when he'd parked beside the pickup truck and gotten out of his car, was in back of the house. From here he could see the barn, of newer vintage than the house and built of wood and metal; several other storage buildings, which might or might not have been garages; a couple of feed storage tanks and some animal pens. These were all off to one side, while directly in back of the house a wide meadow swept down to a creek bed, which was dry now, in September, like most of the Southwest watercourses he was familiar with, and studded with granite outcroppings and copses of still more live oaks. The meadow was dotted with oak trees—not live oaks, but the big, spreading kind—and bordered by a fence rampant with fading sunflowers. A couple of horses and an assortment of brown-and-white goats and some llama-looking creatures occupied the shade provided by the oak trees. Beyond all that, the rolling Texas hills stretched away to distant blue haze.

"Nice," he said to the view's owner as she came to join him. The dog, he noted, was still glued to her side, and the boy had come now to the back-porch door and was watching him intently, arms folded and feet planted firmly a little apart. *Like a sentry*, he thought.

"You should see it in the spring when the bluebonnets are in bloom." It was a pleasant remark, but her face and her eyes reflected no joy or pleasure.

*As if*, Tony thought, *all the light in her life had been snuffed out like a candle's flame.*

She turned and went up the steps to the back door, indicating with a slight movement of her head that he was to follow. Squelching the empathy for her that kept intruding on his objectivity, and with the dog padding silently at his heels, he did, pausing to wipe his feet on the mat outside the door the way his mama had taught him. He entered the kitchen, and the dog squeezed past him and went to assume her Sphinx posture on a rug near the door that led to the rest of the house, making it clear to him his admittance went only this far and no farther.

A wave of his hostess's hand indicated he should sit down at the kitchen table, so he did. He felt as if he'd been called to the principal's office, which had the effect of rendering him, for one of the few times in his life when in the presence of a beautiful woman, at a loss for something to say.

Since he didn't seem to be much good at talking to Brooke, he looked across the table at her son, who had hitched himself halfway onto a chair and was studying him solemnly, with his head propped on his hands. "You're Daniel, right?" Tony held out his hand. "Hi, I'm Tony."

"I know." Daniel ignored the hand and, without

actually pointing, indicated the laptop computer lying open but dormant on the table. "I Googled you."

"Ah." Tony shifted so he was facing the boy more directly, though he was intensely conscious of the kid's mother drilling holes in the back of his head with those dark blue eyes. "Then you know," he said earnestly, "that I've done photo essays of all kinds of animals. Wolves, elephants, gorillas…"

Daniel nodded. "You've been all kinds of places, in wars and disasters and stuff. So how come all of a sudden you want to do a story about one little mountain lion?"

Tony sat back in his chair, and all he could think was, *Wow*.

Behind him he heard, softly, "I'd like to know the answer to that, too."

He turned halfway around in his chair, ready to launch into the story he and Holt had concocted, which he now had no real faith was going to hold up under the scrutiny of these two. "Mrs. Grant—"

Her eyes squinched as if she'd felt a sharp pain. "Oh, please don't call me that. Brooke is fine."

"Okay…Brooke. Actually," he said, glad that this was at least partly true, "I've been interested in doing a story on exotic animal smuggling and illegal breeding for quite a while. Like, what happens to these animals after their owners decide they can't or don't want to take care of them anymore—"

"That's not—" Daniel began, but a gesture from his mother silenced his protest.

Tony glanced at him, then forged ahead into the part of his story that was somewhat less than truthful. "I was doing research—yeah, okay, I Googled—and the news story about what happened to your, uh, with your cougar came up. At that point it was supposed to have been a case of—" he threw the boy a look of apology "—an unprovoked attack by a wild cougar who'd been raised as a pet."

This time it was he who held up a hand to hold off Daniel's furious denial. "So, since I was in Arizona, visiting my mom at the time, and that's right next door by Texas standards, I decided to come and see if you'd let me use your lion as the focus of my story. I didn't know until I got here about…what's been going on."

He sat back, relieved that he could at least end on a note that *was* God's honest truth. "Look, I'm truly sorry. I know this is a bad time for you. But like I said to Daniel, if doing a story on your cougar can help keep her from being put down…"

"Will Lady be on Animal Planet or something like that?" Daniel's face was flushed and eager, though his eyes remained wary.

"Yeah, that's what I'm hoping for. Or National Geographic, maybe. I don't know at this point." He didn't add that if the story was big enough and went the wrong way, it could wind up on some of the crime shows and even on TruTV.

Daniel looked past him and said, "Mom?"

Tony turned to look at her, too, and they both waited for her to say something.

For a long moment she didn't and just stood there leaning against the kitchen sink, with her arms folded, gazing at her son the way he'd seen his own mother do when she couldn't think up a good enough reason to tell him no. Finally, she hitched in a breath—the decision had been made—and Tony held his until she said, "Daniel, why don't you go see if Lady's up for visitors?" When Daniel seemed about to argue, she added in a firmer tone, "We'll be out in a minute. I have some questions I need to ask Mr. Whitehall first."

Daniel slid out of his chair and was out the door in the shot-from-a-cannon manner of little boys everywhere, and the dog rose to her feet, then sat back down and watched him go, clearly torn by this division in her flock. Tony braced himself while Brooke turned her intent gaze his way.

"Mr. Whitehall—"

"Please," he said, with a teasing parody of her own wince, "call me Tony."

She didn't smile—okay, so evidently she wasn't going to be affected by his charm—as she pulled out the chair her son had just vacated. She sat in it, then once again fixed him with that stare.

He looked back at her, trying to look guileless and all too aware that he'd never been much good at guile, anyway. The air around and between him and the woman seemed to quiver with suspense, until he couldn't take it anymore and finally had to break it. "Well, okay, you said you had questions."

"Actually," she said, with a defensive little jerk of her head, "I'm waiting for you. So go ahead—ask it. The question I know you're dying to ask." When Tony just looked at her in a lost kind of way, she gave an impatient wave of her hand. "Oh, come on. Of course, it's

why you're here. Did I or did I not kill my husband?"
She closed her eyes briefly and corrected herself. "*Ex*-
husband. That's what you really want to know. I can
practically hear what's playing inside your head. Did
she really shoot her husband with a tranquilizer gun,
then put him in a cage with a mountain lion, frame the
lion for the killing and arrange it so her nine-year-old
son was the one to find his father's body and provide
her with an alibi?"

"Jeez," Tony said under his breath, unexpectedly
shaken.

She clasped her hands together in front of her and
leaned toward him across the table. "Look, I don't know
if I believe your story about Animal Planet and all that,
but what you told Daniel is true. You *are* in a position
to maybe save an animal we love from being destroyed.
So, I'm willing to let you do your story—or whatever
you call it when it's photographs—as long as you understand it's to be about the cougar and *only* that. Nothing
else. Not one word or picture of me or Daniel—"

He sat back and let out a breath through pursed lips.
"Ma'am, I don't think that's possible. It's your lion.
You and your son raised him, you said. I can't very well
leave you out."

She put a hand over her eyes. "Oh, *hell*. No. I suppose
not." The eyes hit him again, fierce and bright. "You
know what I mean. You are not to make this about what
happened to Duncan. What they say I did. Understand?"
She waited for his nod, then sat back, looking like she'd
just run a race.

She wasn't ready to trust him.

He'd had some experience coaxing wary creatures into an acceptance of him and his cameras, and he realized that was how he'd begun to think of her—as someone who needed to be wooed. Not as he would a beautiful woman, but as if she were one of the shy, wild things he'd stalked and filmed in their natural habitat. That experience had taught him that the way to win such a creature's trust was not to press, not to move too fast, but to hold back and let her come to him.

So, instead of accepting her invitation…demand… challenge…and asking her the questions she'd obviously prepared the answers for, he pushed back from the table and asked softly instead, "Can I see her—your lion?"

"Oh," Brooke said, and he felt he'd won a small victory when she looked taken aback. "Okay. I guess so. Sure."

*Okay, fine.* She led him back down the steps and across the yard to the barn in a grumpy silence, more annoyed with herself than with him. *So I psych myself up to tell you my story, and now you don't want to hear it? Fine with me.*

*So why this odd and completely contrary sense of disappointment?*

*Maybe because…I really do want to tell him. Maybe because I want so desperately for someone to believe me, and I thought maybe, just maybe, this man who isn't from around here and doesn't know Duncan or have any reason to be wary of the local law would listen and believe I'm telling the truth.*

But he didn't seem to want to hear the story from her point of view, which was probably just as well. Her lawyer would have had a fit, anyway.

"Don't you want to get your camera or something?" she asked as they passed his sleek gray sedan, parked alongside her dusty pickup.

"Animals tend to be suspicious of cameras aimed at them," Tony explained, aiming that smile across at her as they walked. "I imagine they must look something like guns—a threat, anyway. I like to let animals—people, too, actually—get used to having me around before I start shooting, photographically speaking."

"I don't think Lady's ever seen a gun," Brooke said, then thought, *Not until a couple of days ago, when somebody shot Duncan with a tranquilizer gun, maybe right in front of her.*

And she wanted so badly to tell him that, to talk to someone about how awful and impossible it was that anyone could think she'd do such a thing.

"Animals seem to have an instinct about things like that," he said. "Somehow they know."

Brooke nodded. After a moment, because the need to talk to someone was just too strong to resist, she said, "Lady's mother was shot and killed, but she was just a blind kitten hidden away in her den at the time, so I don't think she'd have any trauma from that." She glanced over at Tony. "That's how we got her. It was a drought year, and a lot of animals—deer and antelope—had come down from the mountains, looking for food. So, naturally, the predators came, too. And there'd been reports of livestock being killed, and then a hiker was attacked, so the sheriff's department was called in. Duncan and Lonnie—that's his partner—were the ones to find the cougar, and after they shot her, that's when they found out she had cubs. Or kittens. I don't know which one is right, either."

She threw him a suggestion of a smile, one that only hinted, Tony thought, at what a real one would be like. *Glorious.*

"Anyway, they looked for the den, but it was the next day before they found it. By the time they brought them home to me, the babies were weak and dehydrated, and the weakest one—the male—we couldn't save it. We fed Lady with an eyedropper at first—Daniel and I did. Daniel was just a little guy then, but he really did help."

"So…your husband is the one who brought you the cougar?"

"Yeah." She gave a funny little laugh that acknowledged the irony in that, but didn't say the words. "We kept her in the house at first. When she got bigger, she followed Daniel around and wrestled with him like a puppy—or like he was her littermate. She'd stalk him and pounce on him and play fight with him, the way puppies and kittens do. It's the way predators train to catch and kill prey, you know. Duncan always worried she'd hurt Daniel, but she never did—beyond a few scratches and teeth marks and tears in his clothes."

With the dog padding quietly along between them, they went through the center aisle of the barn, between rows of horse stalls and out the other side, into a lane flanked by fenced enclosures. Some of these contained small shelters, which, Tony surmised, were for the goats he'd seen in the meadow pasture. Down at the far end of the lane, he could see a high chain-link fence, like the kind usually used to enclose tennis courts. Daniel was kneeling in the dirt beside the fence, his fingers laced in the wire fabric. Tony's heart began to beat faster when he saw the sleek and tawny shape looming close on the other side, but when he and Brooke and the dog got to the enclosure, the cat had vanished.

"She's shy with strangers," Daniel explained, squinting up at them, and now Tony saw the cat farther out in the compound, standing wary and alert in the shade of an oak tree.

For cougar habitat, the compound ranked among the best he'd seen, with not only trees and brush for cover, but rocky outcroppings for climbing and a piece of the dry streambed running through it. "Nice," he said, and Brooke nodded.

"I had it built when I knew Lady couldn't ever be returned to the wild. Of course, I knew that when she got bigger, she'd become a danger to the other animals."

"Not to mention the people," Tony said, glancing at her. She looked away, but not before he saw a flare of anger in her eyes.

"You may not believe this, but as rough as she was with Daniel when she was little, that's how gentle she is now that she's grown. And with me, too. She's so sweet natured… That's why I can't—" She broke off, shaking her head as she stared through the chain-link fence. After a moment she went on in a voice tight with strain. "Duncan never liked her. And she didn't like him, either. I think they were both afraid of each other. As if…I always wondered if somehow Lady knew he was the one who'd killed her mother. And Duncan…" She paused. "Far-fetched, I know."

"Maybe not," Tony said. "Maybe he had the scent of her mother on him when he first picked her up. Her blood."

Brooke drew a sharp, quivering breath. "Can you get her to come closer?" she asked Daniel.

He shook his head as Tony crouched down beside him. "She doesn't like strangers."

"That's okay," Tony said.

And then there was silence. His pulse pounded in his ears as he stared across the open space between the fence and the oak tree, and from its shelter, the cougar stared back at him. He could hear the hum of insects and the far-off whistle of a hawk…the sound of a car or a tractor starting up somewhere…but, above it all, the beating of his own heart.

And then the distance between him and the cougar seemed to shrink, and the animal's distinctive dark mask grew larger, her vivid yellow eyes glowing like fire.

He heard a soft gasp from close beside him, and an even softer "Sshh…" from somewhere above his head.

He couldn't take his eyes away from that mask… those eyes. And slowly, they came closer, and closer still, until they seemed to fill his entire world, his whole field of vision, the way they had once before, long, long ago.

## Chapter 4

His father had been working cattle in the high country that summer—the high-altitude meadows of the Sierra Nevada. The cow camp had cabins for the hands, so his mother and the four youngest kids—the ones too young to have summer jobs—had joined him for a month toward the end of the roundup season. Branding time. Josie and Anita had been ten and twelve that year, and they liked to go watch the cowboys work the cattle, but Tony and Elena had been too young to be trusted to keep out of the way, so they had to stay in camp with Mama.

Or they were supposed to.

*We're bored, Elena and I, and Mama is busy in the cookhouse, helping the cook make biscuits for dinner, so we decide to go find our own adventures. We'll stay well away from the meadow where the cowboys and the cattle and horses are, we tell each other, so we won't get into trouble.*

*We're walking along, and we come around a big pile of rocks, and there it is, right in front of us. A mountain lion. We freeze, all three of us, and the lion seems as surprised as we are.*

*I can't seem to breathe. Everything inside me has frozen solid. All I can see is the lion's face, with its black mask and big yellow eyes. It seems huge, taller than I am, and I can almost feel its breath on my face. Beside me, Elena whimpers.*

*"Don't move," I whisper without moving my lips. But I feel my sister's hand creep into mine.*

*I don't know how long we stand there, the three of us, staring into each other's eyes. Then, suddenly, the lion twists its body and bounds away over the rocks and is gone.*

*Elena gives a little gasp and looks at me. Her face is pale, and there is moisture on her cheeks. "Don't tell Mama," I say, and she shakes her head, quickly and hard. "We can't tell anyone—ever," I say as she wipes her cheeks with her hands. "If we do, they'll come with guns and shoot it. You have to promise."*

*She nods, sniffs and says, "She didn't hurt us."*

*But she takes my hand again as we walk back to the camp, and I feel a prickling on the back of my neck, as if yellow lion eyes are watching me all the way.*

* * *

"Wow," Daniel said. "She's never done *that* before. Look, Mom. She's not even afraid."

Tony looked up at Brooke and shrugged. "Just got the knack, I guess," he said, making light of it because his chest felt peppery inside and his world still shivered around its edges with the vividness of the memory flashback.

He heard her take a shuddering breath. "Daniel, time for you to get started on your homework. You have some makeup work to do. Don't even think about arguing."

Daniel hurriedly closed his mouth, evidently having been ready to do more than think about it. He let his drooping shoulders and hanging head show how unfair he thought it was, and lumbered off in the loose, disjointed way of disappointed children everywhere. Tony vividly recalled employing the same drama tactics, to roughly the same effect.

"He sure does mind well," he remarked, and she made a dry sound that might have been a laugh.

"He's been on his best behavior since…all this happened." She said it without much expression in her voice but couldn't keep the shadows of everything she'd been through in the recent past from flashing across her face.

Couldn't keep it from Tony, anyway, because he had an eye trained to notice such subtleties. The tension in her facial muscles made his own ache.

Gently, not wanting to distress her more, he finally asked the question she'd already offered to answer. "What happened here?" When she didn't reply immediately, he said, "I promised I wouldn't write or photo-

graph anything about it, and I won't. But you're right—
I would like to know."

He'd meant to leave it there, but she finished for him
as if he hadn't. "Whether you're in the company of a
killer or not?"

She crouched down beside him and put her face close
to the wire and her fingers through it, and the cougar
licked her fingers and butted her head up against the
wire like a house cat wanting to be petted. Tony heard
a peculiar rumbling sound, almost a vibration felt in his
bones rather than heard, and with a small sense of
wonder, he realized the animal was purring.

With her eyes closed, Brooke fought to gain control
of her emotions, wondering why it seemed so tempting
to give in to them here, now, with this strangely charis-
matic and imposing man. She drew in a breath and began.

"I was late getting home from town...."

He listened intently, not interrupting, and when she
was through with her story, she stood up, and so did he.
She looked down at Lady, who, at some point during her
narrative had flopped down at the base of the fence and
was lying stretched out with her back to them, close
enough to touch through the wire. She seemed completely relaxed except for the tip of her tail, which
twitched now and then.

"She seems to have accepted you completely," she
said with a small laugh, because she was in suspense,
wanting to know how he was going to respond. Because
she needed so badly to be believed. "For her to turn her
back on you like this, it means she trusts you."

"What can I say?" he said, showing that incongruous

dimple. Then he cleared his throat, and his voice was abrupt, almost harsh. "Mind if I ask you some questions?"

She shrugged and spread her hands. Not saying the words, but thinking, *What does it matter?* Feeling gray and dismal and hopeless.

"I guess what I don't understand is how they think you could have done this when your—excuse me—when Duncan was already dead when you got here, and Daniel is your witness to that fact. What? Do they think he's lying to protect you?"

She threw him a look, feeling faint touches of warmth and light that were like the first rays of the rising sun on a frosty morning.

"No, actually." She tried to smile and couldn't even manage irony. Fear was a cold chill in her belly and a brassy taste in her throat when she swallowed. "They think I set it all up before I left, before Daniel got home from school. They say I asked Duncan to meet me here, somehow lured him into the compound, shot him with the tranq gun, let Lady out of her cage, *then* went to town to do my shopping. That I never meant for Daniel to be the one to find him, which only happened because the guy at the feed store had lost my order and I was late getting home."

He was frowning, his tawny eyes intent in a way that reminded her oddly of the cougar's eyes.

"So…do you have a tranq gun? The one you're supposed to have used?"

She hissed out a breath. "I do have a tranq gun. *Did.* And that's weird, because it's gone."

"Gone? What do you mean? Like—lost, stolen…"

"All I know is, it's missing. Duncan bought it for me when Lady got big. He was afraid she might attack Daniel—or me, I suppose. He kept it in the tack room, in the barn, so it would be handy in case…in case Lady ever went berserk, I guess." She wiped her eyes with the back of her hand and laughed thickly. "Ironic, huh?" She sniffed and, after a moment, went on. "Anyway, I told the police—uh, sheriff's department detectives, you know—where it was, and they said it wasn't there. They had a warrant and searched the whole place for it, and so far they haven't found it. Which, as far as they're concerned, only proves their theory, that I did it before I left for town, took the gun with me and disposed of it somewhere on the way."

"I don't know," Tony said in a slow and thoughtful way. "It all sounds pretty circumstantial."

"Yes. But don't forget, I also have motive. Duncan was contesting our custody agreement. He wanted full custody of Daniel. And this being a county in which the good-ol' boys system governs just about everything, he actually might have won." She struggled again with the smile. "And don't they always suspect the husband or wife first? Especially—" she drew a shivering breath "—when there's nobody else to suspect. I mean, who else *could* it be, right?"

She looked at him, and he looked back at her, not saying anything. She thought he looked shaken. *Because he thinks I'm a murderer? Or because he sees, as I do, how hopeless it is…*

"So," she said when the silence had stretched as far as it could, "do you still want to do your story when the odds are I really am a cold-blooded killer?" To her own ears her voice sounded as thin and brittle as she felt. As if the wrong word would shatter her into a million pieces. She watched him closely, waiting for it…

But he only said, "Okay if I come back tomorrow? Looks like Lady's okay with me, so I don't see why I can't start shooting." He wasn't smiling, but it seemed to her—she wasn't imagining it?—that his eyes were kind.

She let out the breath she didn't know she'd been holding. "Tomorrow's fine," she said, not smiling, either. But once again she felt it—that faint touch of warmth.

"I don't think she did it," Tony said to Holt at the diner that evening. He had just put in his order for the deluxe Black Angus cheeseburger and was trying not to think about all the stuff his sisters had just been preaching to him about bad fats and red meat and cholesterol. He shook his head and reached for his beer. "But I'm not sure I'm gonna be able to stay objective on the subject."

Holt leaned back against the booth's red plastic upholstery and draped one long arm along the top edge of it and gave him a narrow-eyed gaze that reminded Tony of Clint Eastwood—minus the stump of cigar. "Why's that?"

Tony shrugged. "Well, shoot, man, she's my best friend's baby sister. Of course, I *want* her to be innocent."

It was enough of a reason to give Holt, but in his heart he knew it wasn't the only one.

He didn't know why, but he couldn't get the lady out of his mind. Images kept flashing through his head like snapshots in a slide show: a work-worn hand resting on the head of a huge, shaggy fawn-and-white dog; laugh lines at the corners of smoky blue eyes filled with tears; a head with spiky blond hair shooting every which way out of a haphazard ponytail, leaning against one side of a chain-link fence, with a mountain lion's head butting against it from the other; a pair of long, slim legs in blue jeans just inches away from his shoulder, folding up to lower a long, slim body down next to him, so close he could feel the heat of it.

Okay, so he was aware of her as a woman. He liked women. Especially beautiful ones. But he'd never had one get into his head like this one had, not in so short a time.

He drank beer, paused, then frowned and said, "The thing is, it doesn't look like she could be. I mean, it all points to her being the only one who could have done it. Circumstantial, sure, but add to that a good motive and the fact that she's the ex-spouse—I mean, hell, *I'd* have arrested her."

"But you don't think she did it."

"No, I don't. Call it a gut feeling, I guess." At least he hoped it was his gut he was feeling, and not some other part of his anatomy, the one known to be considerably less reliable in its judgments.

"Well, okay then," said Holt, and then they both leaned back to allow the waitress—a buxom, fortyish woman with shocking red hair—to deliver their dinner plates.

"Thanks, Shirley—looks great," Holt told her with a wink and a smile, and she smiled back at him, gave her fanny a little wiggle, said, "Eat up, hon. You need some meat on your bones," as she winked at Tony and sashayed off.

"Okay, so let's go from there." Holt picked up a bottle of steak sauce and studied his plate for a moment before applying generous amounts to his burger and passing the bottle on to Tony. "Let's assume she didn't do it. So…who did?" He picked up his burger, bit into it, looked at Tony and raised his eyebrows as he chewed.

Tony gave a bark of laughter without much amusement in it.

Holt leaned toward him, and Tony thought again of Clint Eastwood. "No, look here. It's a matter of logic. If she didn't do it, someone else did. So, we have to think who could have done the things she's supposed to have done. Take it one thing at a time." He held up a finger. "One, the victim was inside the cougar's cage. How did he get there? You said Brooke told you her ex was afraid of the lion. So, would he go in there by himself? Not likely. Not willingly, anyway. Which means somebody either had to put him in there after he was tranqed, or somehow enticed him in while he was still mobile."

"He was a big man, from what I understand," Tony said, beginning to get into it now himself. "And there were no drag marks, at least that I could see or anyone mentioned. Brooke couldn't have put him in the cage herself, I don't think."

"So," said Holt, with a shrug, after another bite and chew, "either it was somebody bigger than the victim, strong enough to carry him, or somebody he trusted enough to go into the cougar's pen with. That's not likely to be an ex-wife he's in a custody battle with, seems to me." He held up a hand. "Actually, that should have been point number two. Number one, what was he doing at his ex's ranch in the first place? His vehicle was there, parked on a dirt road that ran around the back of Brooke's property. A road that passes pretty close by where the cougar's pen is. I've been doing some scouting of my own," he explained when Tony started to ask how he knew that. "So, that's a big question. Why was he there? If he was there to see Brooke, wouldn't he just go up the driveway to the house? We have to assume he met someone there—the person who killed him, right? Who would he go there to meet? And why?"

"You have to think they—whoever the other party or parties were—they were up to no good," Tony said, chewing thoughtfully. "Otherwise, like you say, why not go on up to the house?"

"Right. Then there's the matter of the weapon."

"The tranquilizer gun." Tony nodded. "Which Brooke says was kept in the tack room in the barn, a room that wasn't locked. And now it's missing."

"Okay," said Holt, leaning back with beer bottle in hand. "Who knew about the gun? For starters, the man who bought it—Duncan Grant."

Tony was frowning. "Let's get this straight. Duncan Grant comes to his ex-wife's ranch when she's not home, parks where he won't be seen, meets some person or persons unknown, most likely male, gets the tranquilizer gun from the tack room—or tells his partners where it is and they take it—and somehow he winds up shot with it and left inside a cougar's compound to die. Then whoever the unknown killer is, he takes the gun and drives away, leaving a nine-year-old boy to discover his father's body, and the lion and the ex to take the blame."

Holt nodded. "That about sums it up."

Tony pushed his plate away with about a third of his burger still on it, having pretty much lost his appetite. "And it explains the dog," he said.

"The dog?"

"Yeah. Brooke's got a giant dog—some kind of sheepdog, I think. Very protective. I don't think she'd have allowed a stranger onto the place, but if it was Duncan and somebody he trusted—"

"Like a friend."

"Right," Tony said.

Then both he and Holt went silent as the diner's door whooshed open and a group of men wearing brown Stetsons and tan shirts came in together, bantering and laughing in the confident, swaggering manner of men who know they own their little corner of the universe.

Tony watched them until they'd settled into a big corner booth near the front of the diner, then turned back to Holt. He felt chilled. "And Duncan's friends are probably mostly gonna be…"

"Cops," said Holt.

Brooke was finishing up the morning chores when she heard a car drive up to the house. She didn't realize until she saw that it wasn't Tony Whitehall's sedan how much she'd been looking forward to his coming.

But it was a sheriff's department SUV. She stood in the big barn doorway and watched it come up the lane and stop beside her pickup, and she felt afraid. It was a cold, sick, queasy kind of fear, a fear that she hadn't felt in a very long time and had hoped she'd forgotten.

*I'm afraid, because I know something bad is about to happen to me, and I know that I am powerless to do anything to stop it, and that there's no one I can turn to for help. I feel dirty and small, and I'm trembling inside, but I know I have to be strong....*

The SUV's door opened and Lonnie Doyle got out. Hilda didn't go trotting out, with her tail wagging, to meet him, although she knew him well from all the times he'd been there with Duncan. Instead, she sat at Brooke's feet, close to her side, trembling a little, as if she, too, was afraid.

"Hey, Brooke," Lonnie said, sauntering toward her, wearing a big smile, as if he'd never made threats against her and her pet cougar, as if he had the right to still call himself her friend just because he was Duncan's. As if he had every right to be there, on her place, which of course, he did, she reminded herself, because he was The Law.

"Lonnie," said Brooke, without a nod or smile.

"Just thought I'd stop by, see how you're doin'." He had the grace to at least *look* a little awkward, although he didn't take off his hat to be polite. Probably, she thought, because it was a big part of what gave him his authority. His power.

"I'm doing okay." Her hand had come to rest on Hilda's silky head, and that gave her a small measure of comfort.

"How's Daniel?"

"He's fine. In school right now."

"Good…good…" His small eyes gazed past her, through the barn and off toward where the animal pens were. Where Lady was. Where Duncan had died. She saw his jaw clench.

Before he could say anything, she asked in a flat voice, "What do you want, Lonnie?"

His eyes flicked at her, then away, and he shifted his stance and folded his arms in a way he maybe meant to be ingratiating but somehow just felt intimidating instead. "Uh, look, Brooke, about the other day. If I came on too strong…" He coughed, and Brooke thought, *My God, is he trying to* apologize? Then he seemed to draw himself together, and the intimidation was back— definitely—as he went on. "Look, Dunk was my best friend—my partner. What that cat did to him. Hell, I would have shot him—"

"Her," Brooke corrected softly, but he didn't seem to hear.

"—if Al hadn't stopped me. I'm glad he did, because I wouldn't want to do that to the boy. To Danny. I'm sorry if I upset him. But, Brooke, you need to understand, that cat is a killer. For your own sake, and the safety of your boy, you need to let that animal go. Let animal control take it and put it down." When she would have protested, he held up a finger, like a teacher lecturing a class of small, unruly children, and moved closer to her, hemming her in. "Look, all you need to do is read the paper, watch TV. There was that case in Florida where two cheetahs turned on their keeper, tore her up good. And then the guy in Las Vegas. What was his name? Anyway, you got no business keeping a dangerous animal like that on your place when you've got a kid to think about."

"Thank you for your concern," Brooke said coldly. "If that's what you came to tell me, you've told me. So, if you don't mind, I really do have work to do."

"Look, I'm just trying to look out for you and Danny. Dunk was my best friend. It's the least I can do."

She felt a dangerous impulse to laugh. But he was standing too close to her, making her feel claustrophobic and, although she couldn't have explained why, *afraid*. It suddenly seemed important to placate him, and that impulse, too, brought back memories she wished she could forget.

She drew a steadying breath. "Lonnie, that's kind of you. But I don't need any help. Really. I've been getting along fine on my own for two years. Daniel and I will be just…fine."

Something glittered in his little blue eyes and quivered around the corners of his mouth, and Brooke thought about what Mr. Henderson had told her, and of all the evidence and suspicion against her, and for a moment she actually thought she might throw up. She felt clammy and cold, and there was a humming in her ears. She couldn't breathe.

Then the spell broke, and instead of humming, she heard the growl of a car making its way up the lane. She felt warm again, and not afraid.

"Who the hell is that?" Lonnie asked, as if he had a right to know. He was scowling, watching the gray sedan pull around and park on the other side of Brooke's pickup.

Brooke drew a breath that quivered with relief and a strange, unanticipated gladness. "Oh," she said in an offhand way, "it's just a reporter. He's doing a story about Lady." She folded her arms and smiled, enjoying the way Lonnie jerked back in surprise. "He's with *National Geographic,* I think. Or Animal Planet—one of those."

His lips curled in a sneer. "Yeah? Well, if you think that's gonna save that cat, think again. He's a killer, and I can guarantee you the judge is gonna see it that way, too, so you tell your Animal Planet big shot he's got until the hearing next week to get his story, because after that the cat is history. Count on it."

He stabbed a finger at her for emphasis as he turned and started for his vehicle, then abruptly turned back, smiling in a way that didn't even try to be friendly. "Oh—forgot to tell you. Just thought you'd like to know, we haven't found the tranq gun yet. Still looking for it, though."

Why did that sound like a threat? Brooke thought as she watched him stride away, barely acknowledging Tony as he passed him by.

She saw Tony pause for a moment to look back at Lonnie, wondering at his rudeness, maybe. When he came on, loaded down with his cameras and bags, he caught her eye, and she saw his tough, bulldog face break into its oddly sweet smile. Once again, that peculiar warmth came over her, along with reassurance, an overwhelming sense that she was safe, now. Because he was here.

Tony felt the animosity as he and the other man passed each other, a wave of something so tangible he could almost see it, smell it, like the smoke from a particularly nasty cigar.

He turned to watch the deputy get into his official sheriff's department vehicle, then continued on, frowning. But when he saw Brooke's face, and that she looked pale and scared, there was something about that and the look in her eyes that affected him in unfamiliar ways. He considered himself a nonviolent person, one much more inclined to make love than war, but he felt a sudden surprising urge to inflict great bodily harm on the individual who had put that fear in this woman's eyes.

He summoned the most reassuring smile he could muster and felt a strange lifting beneath his heart when she smiled back, even though her smile didn't reach as far as her eyes. "What's wrong? What's a deputy sheriff doing here?" he asked her, aware that his own bravado was equivalent to that of a nine-year-old's, secure in the knowledge that the school-yard bully had already departed the field of battle.

She shook her head, made a gesture, making light of it all. "Oh, that's just Lonnie." She took a breath. "Duncan's partner."

"Ah," said Tony. He glanced down at the dog, who was in her usual position beside Brooke, but panting lazily and gazing after the departing SUV, evidently not in the least concerned about Tony's presence there. He was remembering what Holt had said about Duncan's friends most likely being other cops. "He's…a friend, then?"

She gave a high, humorless laugh. "Not mine."

He could see her struggling with it, not sure whether she could trust him, afraid to say too much. But, of course, she already had told him a lot, much more than she probably realized. He was good at reading faces.

"Gotcha," he said, turning as if to walk on toward the barn's wide, open entrance, as if he didn't need her to say another word. Which, in the contrary way of people—women especially, in his experience—gave her permission to say what was on her mind.

"They grew up together, Lonnie and Duncan," she said as she came to walk beside him. "I swear, as long as I knew Duncan Grant, wherever he was, I could count on Lonnie not being far away. They played high school football together. Just generally raised hell together. Then they both joined the sheriff's department and went off to learn to be cops together, which kind of surprised everyone, I think. Most people around here probably thought they'd wind up in the same jail cell—together."

"Stands to reason he'd take his buddy's death hard," said Tony. "Sounds like they must have been really close."

She tilted her head in a thoughtful way. "Close? Yeah, they were…I guess. But the funny thing is, they didn't always get along. Most of the time, in fact. Those two probably had more bare-knuckle brawls than any two best buddies in the state of Texas, which is saying a lot. I guess maybe they were more like brothers who didn't see eye to eye most of the time."

*Cain and Abel were brothers, too,* Tony thought. But he said, "What about you?"

"I never did care much for him," she said in a diffident way, watching the ground in front of her. Then she threw him a look and a wry smile. "Can't stand the man, if you want to know the truth. And I'm sure the feeling is mutual. Lonnie being single, I imagine he didn't much like losing his good ol' drinkin' and hell-raisin' buddy—not that I noticed Duncan's lifestyle or priorities changed much after we got married. Or even after Daniel was born, for that matter." She went back to looking at the ground, forehead furrowed. "That's why I can't understand—"

"What?" he prompted when she paused, but she shook her head.

"Nothing. Really." She gave a soft, embarrassed laugh. "I can't imagine why I'm even tellin' you all this. Particularly after I said you couldn't do one little bit of your story about me or Daniel. I still do mean that, by the way." She gave him the last in a warning tone, but with a new lightness in her attitude that made it seem almost like banter.

He looked over at her as they strolled, unhurried, down the lane between animal pens, with the dog trotting on ahead of them. Brooke had her fingertips tucked in the pockets of her jeans and her face lifted to the warm September sun. Her straight, layered, sun-streaked hair was twisted up in an artless style and fastened to the back of her head with a wide metal clip, leaving pieces sticking out and waving around her head in a way that was whimsical but oddly attractive. The camera shutter in his mind went *click*.

"No story," he said. "Just interested. What don't you understand?"

Again, she hesitated, then let out a surrendering breath. "Why Duncan even wanted custody of Daniel. I don't think Lonnie understood it, either. I would think Daniel would just have gotten in his way."

"What about Daniel? How does he feel about it?"

"The custody battle?" Her face was suddenly a study in anger…bitterness…pain. "He doesn't want to live with his dad, that's for sure." She threw him a look and quickly added, "Oh, don't get me wrong. Daniel loves his father. *Loved.*" She closed her eyes briefly, and he saw her throat struggle with a swallow. "But—" and her voice had gone harsh and soft "—he'll *never* forget what that man did to me."

Tony didn't want to ask, but of course he had to. "What did he do?"

They'd reached the cougar's high wire enclosure. Brooke halted and, with a jerky, angry gesture, lifted her hair away from her forehead to show him the white scar running into her scalp. She turned to him and tried, without success, to smile. "That's just the one that shows."

# Chapter 5

Brooke wasn't prepared for the emotions that flashed across Tony Whitehall's rugged face. What she saw there made her feel validated, and at the same time, oddly, *scared*.

"He hit you?" He asked it very softly, not looking at her now. *Carefully* not looking at her, she thought, and squinting slightly, as if the sight of her might hurt his eyes.

Shaken, she tried to backpedal. Tried to laugh, make it sound like less than it was. "Damn. I guess that just gives me more of a motive to kill him, doesn't it?"

"It would have," Tony said, and to her relief, his voice sounded more like his normal voice. He was looking at her again, too, and the warmth was back in his eyes. "But you divorced him instead. Seems strange you didn't kill him back then, when you had good reason to…"

She felt shaky, trembly inside. Wrapping her arms around herself, trying without success to stop the feeling, she looked across the compound to where Lady was lying in the shade of an oak tree, ignoring them. "I guess it's a fairly common practice among cops."

"No excuse."

"No, but I have a feeling his dad was the same way. So maybe he didn't know how else to be."

He threw her a look, angry now. "What are you doing? Apologizing for him? He beat you. The woman he's supposed to love and protect. How can any man justify that? How can any woman put up with it? My mother would have killed my dad in a heartbeat if he'd ever laid a hand on her in anger. Guaranteed."

Brooke had no answer for that. After a moment she said flatly, "I guess you were lucky, weren't you?" And she walked away, once more feeling alone.

Tony watched her go, with the big dog trotting along beside her. He was wondering if there was some way he could take back what he'd said. Make it up to her, at least. Cut his tongue out, maybe?

Then he felt a moment's intense and familiar longing, thinking of his dad's rough, gnarled cowboy's hands, hands that had been hard as iron but never any other way but gentle when they'd touched his children or his wife. When he was home, how the kids—the little ones—used to love to climb all over him, messing up his hair, tugging his mustache, taking off his cowboy hat and putting it on their own heads…. And Mama, standing a little way off, just smiling in a quiet way. Like she was proud of him, Tony thought, even though he'd never brought home much money, for sure not enough for the eleven kids he'd given her to raise. Eleven kids that had somehow all gone to college, which he knew was mostly thanks to Mama, but still, it was his dad he missed with an ache that never seemed to get smaller, even though it had been fifteen years since the heart attack that killed him.

"You're a jerk, you know that?" he told himself out loud.

But he was watching the cougar now and thinking about the job, and the fact that if he was going to be able to get any decent shots of the animal, he was pretty much going to have to go inside the compound with it. Again, he flashed back to that day when he'd come face-to-face with a wild mountain lion, and the pact he and Elena had made afterward. He could see the tear tracks on her face and could hear her whisper, "She didn't hurt us."

He looked at the gate in the high chain-link fence, which was fastened with a chain but not locked. He looked at the lion, still lying on her side out there in the shade of the oak tree, gazing off into the distance. Maybe sleeping?

*Are you dreaming, Lady? Dreaming about the days when this land belonged to you, and there was no one to contest your mastery of all your surveyed?*

Ignoring him, anyway.

Scolding himself for his cowardice—and telling himself he could always beat a hasty retreat if the cat made a move toward him—Tony closed his eyes briefly, then unhooked the chain. It made what seemed like a hellishly loud noise.

Out in the compound, the cougar turned her head to watch him but didn't get up.

"Nice kitty, kitty. Nice Lady..." he said on an exhaled breath as he slowly opened the gate and slipped into the lion's den.

"You know what I was thinking?" Tony said to Holt after he'd told him about it that evening at the diner. "That it felt wrong, that animal having a fence around it. You know what I mean? The buffalo, the wolf, the lion and the grizzly bear—we've crowded them off their land, stolen it from them. Like the white man stole it from the Indians—my people."

Holt's eyes had crinkled up at the corners, but he swallowed the bite of steak he was working on before he said, with exaggerated seriousness, "Your people? How much Native American are you?"

Tony shrugged. "Okay, my mama's about three-quarters Apache—maybe half, I don't know—so that makes me less than half, but still. Doesn't change what happened—to the natives or to the animals."

"No," Holt said agreeably. "So, the cat didn't attack you, I gather?"

"Didn't bat an eye. I was busy getting out all my equipment, and she just lay there, twitching her tail once in a while. Mind you, I didn't try to go and pet her, or anything. But she pretty much ignored me the whole time I was in the pen with her. Even rolled over on her back and put her paws in the air and squirmed around—just like a big kitty cat, you know?" He paused to shake his head and let out a breath, remembering the sense of awe he'd felt. "It was...pretty amazing." He picked up his fork and pointed it at Holt. "And if you ask me, it makes it pretty hard to believe that animal attacked somebody. Not without some serious provocation."

Holt pushed his plate aside and sat back. His eyes had that Clint Eastwood glitter. "You said that deputy—Lonnie Doyle—made some threats?"

"Sure sounded like it. I was getting my equipment out of the car at the time, so I didn't hear everything he said, but he seems to have a real hate for that cat. And no great love for Brooke, either." He paused, giving himself time to control his voice before he added, "She's afraid of him, I know that."

"And he and Duncan Grant were best friends...." He left it dangling.

Tony sat and looked at him for a long moment, not saying anything. Then he shook his head...made a jerky gesture of rejection. "Nah. I mean, fistfights is one thing, but to shoot a guy with a tranquilizer gun and leave him to die in a lion's cage? I can't see it. What possible reason would the guy have to kill his best friend?"

"It happens," Holt said. He leaned forward again, arms folded on the tabletop. "And when it does, it's usually over one of two things. A woman or money."

"Well, it's not a woman," Tony said. "Not this woman, anyway."

"So," said Holt, picking up his beer, "that leaves money."

* * *

Brooke had stopped what she was doing—raking old bedding straw out of the horses' stalls—to watch Daniel and Tony down in the pasture. As always, Daniel was surrounded by a motley herd of animals—horses, goats and alpacas. Tony stood close by and was obviously trying to ignore the goats nibbling at his pockets and shirtsleeves, looking for treats. Hilda was off down by the creek, nosing around, looking to scare up a squirrel or a rabbit to chase. A warm September breeze was blowing, bringing with it the smell of autumn and the sound of voices.

Daniel's husky alto, first. "Yeah, but that's just the way alpacas chew, see? They're really tame, too—come on, you can pet 'em, if you want to…feel how soft their wool is…"

And Tony, his warm laughter soft as the alpacas' wool on her ears. "You sure do know a lot about animals."

Daniel, with a self-conscious shrug. "Yeah. I'm going to be a veterinarian. It takes lots of college, though. Almost as much as a real doctor. And I have to take a lot of math, which doesn't make me very happy…"

"Hey, vets *are* real doctors. Especially nowdays."

"I meant *people* doctors. *You* know. Actually, it's harder to be a vet, 'cause animals can't tell you what's wrong with them. So you have to be twice as smart to figure it out."

"True. But I think you're going to make one helluva vet—oh, shoot. Sorry about that."

"That's okay. My mom says hell sometimes. Worse stuff than that, too. I already know I'm not s'posed to say it, you know, because I'm a kid…."

Brooke let go of a bubble of laughter, and when she

put a hand up to stifle it, she was surprised to discover some moisture on her face as well. She brushed it away hastily, but it was harder to dispatch the ache of yearning that had come over her suddenly. A yearning she couldn't put a name to, but that whispered, softly as the breeze, *Oh, if only...if only...*

Down in the pasture, Tony took off the Arizona Diamondbacks cap he'd put on to protect his scalp and wiped his head with his sleeve as he squinted at the lowering Texas sun.

"Speaking of math..." he said, and Daniel groaned.

"Don't say it. I know...I have homework."

Knowing how much he'd hate it, Tony resisted an urge to tousle the boy's thick blond hair and instead laid his hand on one sturdy shoulder. "Just keep your eye on the prize. Keep telling yourself it's what it takes to be a vet someday. You'll get through it."

"Yeah, but...I wish..." He didn't finish his sentence, but walked with his head down, in his dejected slouch, as they made their way slowly up the slope.

Feeling helpless, Tony gave the kid's shoulder a squeeze. While he was racking his brain for something to say to cheer him up, Daniel kicked at a clump of dried horse apples and said fervently, "I wish you didn't always have to go."

*Oh, hell.* He hadn't expected that. It was like getting slugged in the stomach when he wasn't prepared for it; it took his breath away.

"Hey," he said softly. And then, after a little cough that was supposed to mask how moved he was, he added, "I'll be back tomorrow."

"I know…."

"And," he added, as inspiration struck, "you can always call me, you know. Anytime."

Daniel's head came up, and smoke-blue eyes—his mother's eyes—shone bright in his flushed face. "Really?"

"Sure," Tony said, rubbing at the persistent peppery itch in his nose. "Uh…let's see. Okay, I know. My cell phone number's on that card I gave your mom. Still have it?"

"Yeah—I think. Yes." He was nodding eagerly, making the standing-up strands of his hair bob. "Mom has it. I'll ask her."

"Well, then, there you go. Call me whenever you feel like it."

Tony hauled in a breath and was grinning in the goofy, relieved way of a man who'd managed to come through a scary moment unscathed. He gave the kid's shoulder one final squeeze and watched him shoot off in the direction of the house at a pace that was only a memory for anybody past twenty. He was feeling pretty good about the way he'd handled things with the boy, until he looked up, and there was Brooke looking back at him. And there *he* was, feeling like he'd been socked in the stomach again.

She was standing in the doorway to one of the horse stalls, one hand leaning on the half-open bottom section of the Dutch door, the other holding a propped-up pitchfork. Her face was pink and sweaty, and wisps of her hair clung to her forehead and cheeks like wet feathers. She ducked her head to wipe her face on the arm braced on the door, and when she looked back at him, her expression was…vulnerable, he thought, so vulnerable it made his heart sore. And at the same time, the lift to her chin seemed defiant—even angry.

"Don't make promises you can't keep," she said in a hard, clipped voice.

"I don't think I did," Tony said carefully as he angled across the pasture to join her. "But, hey, look, I'm sorry if I was out of line."

She made an impatient gesture and looked down at her feet, clad in clumpy knee-high boots. "It's not that." She took a breath and shot him a fierce, bright look, one he'd seen on his own mother's face and knew very well: Mama Bear protecting her cub. "He's very vulnerable right now. He just lost his dad." She paused, and to the fierceness was added an intriguing layer of something he could only think must be embarrassment. "He's… For some reason, he's developing an attachment to you. But you're only here for a couple of days. What is he supposed to do when you're gone?"

To his astonishment and dismay, the words "I'm not going anywhere" popped into his head and almost— *almost*—came out of his mouth. Thank God he stopped himself in time. What was he thinking? She was right. He was only here for a couple more days. He'd probably already got enough cougar photos to fill an article for *National Geographic*, and enough video for a couple of Animal Planet shows as well. He couldn't tell her his real reason for hanging around, of course.

*Which is to somehow get her cleared of murder*

*charges and reunite her with her long-lost brothers, after*
*which my job here will be done and I'll be long gone.*
   *Right?*
   "Gotcha," he said, and then added, frowning earnestly, "I understand. I hear what you're saying." He said some other basically meaningless stuff—he wasn't sure what—but he hoped he'd assured the mama bear that he wasn't planning to inflict emotional harm on her cub.

   He was pretty sure he said "Good-bye" and "See you tomorrow" in there somewhere, too, and a short time later found himself sitting behind the wheel of his rental car. He sat there staring through the windshield and listening to his heart thump faster than it should while images flashed through his mind: A grubby little boy's hand gently stroking soft, thick alpaca wool…bright little boy's eyes gazing eagerly up at him. Sweat-damp feathers of blond hair sticking to a lovely woman's forehead and cheekbones—bones that would still be lovely when they were ninety. Nothing new there—he had a photographer's mind. What was making his pulse rate climb and his sweat grow clammy were the images that were drawn from pure fantasy: his hands stroking those feathers of hair back from that lovely woman's face…his lips kissing her sweat-damp brow…and then her cheeks…her mouth.…

   He huffed out an explosive breath, along with some blasphemy his mama definitely wouldn't have approved of, started up the car and drove—too fast—down the lane and onto the FM road that would take him back to town and sanity. He hoped.

   It wasn't until he'd calmed down some and his pulse had resumed a more normal rhythm that he thought to check his rearview mirror. That was when he saw the sheriff's patrol car behind him.

His heart gave a guilty kick, the way it probably did for most people when they looked up and saw a law-enforcement vehicle in their mirror. He swore out loud and tried to think whether he'd disobeyed any traffic laws while in his state of lapsed consciousness, all the while making sure to hold steady just under the speed limit. After a while, though, when the lights on top of the SUV didn't start flashing, it occurred to him to wonder why a deputy sheriff would be following him at all, because in his—admittedly limited—law-enforcement experience, the sheriff's department seldom bothered to police traffic-law violators.

And this guy seemed to be sticking to him like glue.

*Well, that's weird,* he thought. He tried to see who was behind the wheel of the SUV, but the windshield showed him only a reflection of the sky, a dusky slate splashed with clouds and just beginning to reveal the amber and gold tints of impending sunset. For reasons he couldn't quite explain, his heart rate had kicked into high again.

The SUV followed him when he made the turn onto the main highway. At the first stoplight heading into town, where the highway widened into four lanes, it pulled up beside him on the left, crowding him just a little more than it needed to. The window rolled slowly down, and a fleshy face wearing aviator sunglasses and topped with a brown Stetson swiveled toward him. For a long, long minute, those dark, blank shades stared at him. Just stared.

Then…the light turned green, the window rode up and the SUV pulled away.

After another sharp exhalation and some more blasphemy, Tony drove on, too.

"I hate to admit it, but it spooked me," he said to Holt a little while later, as they waited for their dinners—they were both having the barbecue tonight, which was on special and which Shirley had assured them was the best in town, if not in all of West Texas. "It sure as hell *felt* like a threat—or a warning, maybe. The only thing I can't figure out is *why*."

"The fact that you've been spending quite a bit of time with a woman suspected of killing one of their own might have something to do with it," Holt said mildly.

Tony frowned. "I wish I could have gotten a better look at the guy. I *think* it was the one I ran into at Brooke's place yesterday—Lonnie Doyle—you know? The dead cop's partner and supposed best friend. Hard to tell for sure, between the hat and the shades. He'd be my first choice for—"

"Speak of the devil," Holt said, without moving his lips.

Three deputies, including Lonnie Doyle, had just come into the diner, not really swaggering, not exactly talking, but somehow taking up more than their fair allotment of oxygen and space, it seemed to Tony. He and Holt watched silently and without seeming to as the three took their usual corner booth, and even without looking directly, it was impossible to miss the glances the lawmen aimed their way.

Shirley went over to the deputies, carrying three mugs and a pot of coffee, and Tony and Holt picked up their own coffee mugs and exchanged looks of silent warning. Tony felt a curious crawling sensation on the back of his neck and wondered if it was the same primitive reflex that made a wolf's hackles rise.

A moment later, Shirley came out of the kitchen, carrying two platters of barbecue, and at the same time, Lonnie Doyle slid out of the corner booth and began to stroll, unhurried, past the row of booths lining the outside wall of the diner, timing it so that he arrived at Tony and Holt's booth about the same time their dinner did. He stood there, with one hand on the back of the booth near Tony's shoulder and the other on his belt, heavy with the cops' usual gear, including weapon, and his barrel chest puffed out. He'd positioned himself so he was blocking Shirley's path, leaving her standing there with the two heavy platters in her hand, and looking uncertain and maybe a little scared.

Tony didn't often lose his temper, but he could feel it rising like the mercury on a blistering hot Arizona day.

"Know what, Shirl? I think my friends here have decided they'd like those ribs to go," Lonnie drawled, staring down at Tony, with his lips curled to one side in a bad imitation of an Elvis Presley sneer.

Tony opened his mouth to give that the reply he thought it deserved, but before he could get a word out, Holt kicked him under the table and said to the waitress, quietly and with a reassuring smile, "Thanks, darlin'. And, if it's not too much trouble, would you mind throwing in a couple pieces of that apple pie?"

Shirley turned without a word and went back to the kitchen.

Lonnie slapped the back of the booth in a business-concluded kind of way. Then, as if it was only an afterthought, he turned back to say in a soft undertone only they would hear, "You might want to watch who you get friendly with, you hear? In this town we don't take kindly to folks who kill cops. And that goes for critters, too." Then he tipped his hat in a parody of politeness and went sauntering back to his buddies, calling good-natured greetings and friendly insults to a couple of other diners on the way.

Too mad to say a coherent word, Tony stared narrow-eyed, across the table at Holt, who locked his gaze with his in a silent warning as he picked up his coffee and drank. A moment later, Shirley came hurrying up, with two plastic bags containing to-go boxes and an assortment of napkins and plastic utensils.

"Guys, I'm really sorry," she muttered under her breath. "I don't want any trouble with those guys, you know?"

"Neither do we," Holt said. "Don't worry about it—not your fault."

As Tony reached for his wallet, Shirley made a quick, furtive gesture of refusal. "That's okay. You can pay me tomorrow—next time you're in. And," she added as an angry flush rose to her cheeks, "the pie's on the house."

Outside, in the cool September evening, Tony clamped his Diamondbacks' cap on his head and let out a string of cusswords he didn't use but once in a blue moon, concluding with, "What the hell was that?"

"Looks like we've struck somebody's nerve," Holt said, sounding almost cheerful.

"Yeah, well, it reminds me of one of those movies—you know, about the poor out-of-towner who wanders into some small town ruled by a corrupt all-powerful sheriff...."

They'd come in Holt's new rental car. While he unlocked it and put his dinner in the backseat, Tony went around to the passenger side and did the same. When they were both settled in the front seats, Holt sat for a moment without starting the engine. Then he looked over at Tony and said, "Might be time we make another try at getting in touch with Cory or Sam. Maybe they've got some connections with the feds...."

Tony nodded grimly. "Sam does, for sure."

"I think," said Holt as he turned the ignition key, "we're going to need some outside help on this one."

It wasn't often Tony was awakened by a ringing cell phone. It happened so seldom, in fact, that it took him awhile to figure out what it was. He opened his eyes and discovered it was still dark—relatively, which didn't mean much in a motel room with the curtains drawn.

In the twin bed next to his, Holt was stirring. "Is that yours or mine?" came the sleep-husky voice.

Tony swore. "Mine, I think." He groped for the offending instrument on the nightstand, at the same time trying to get a look at the alarm clock, which was turned just enough so he couldn't see the lighted numbers. He found the phone, thumbed it on and croaked a raspy "H'lo?"

"Tony?"

He sat up, if not wide awake, at least adrenaline-charged. *"Daniel?"*

"You said I could call you, right?" The voice was a whisper, but hoarse with urgency. "I mean…if I needed you, or something…"

"Yeah, yeah…so what's—is something wrong? What time is it, anyway?"

"Not that early. Almost time for the school bus. But I'm not going. Tony, um…can you come over? Right now?"

"Now?" He threw the covers back and got his feet on the floor. His heart rate had kicked into high gear, and there was a cold knot forming in his belly. "What's goin' on, son? Is your mom—"

"No—she doesn't know I'm calling. But I didn't know what else to do. They're taking Lady. I think they're gonna kill her."

"What do you mean, kill her? They can't, not without a court order. There hasn't even been a hearing yet." He glanced at Holt, who was up and heading for the bathroom.

"Yeah, but Lonnie and a bunch of other deputies—some of 'em I don't even know—they're here right now, and they have a pickup with a big cage—it's from animal control, or something—and they said they're taking Lady and they're holding her until the hearing. But I think they're going to do something to her. I know they want to kill her because they think she killed my dad after…you know. My mom—"

"Yeah. I know. Okay, listen. You sit tight, you hear me? I'll be right there. You think you and your mom can hold 'em off until I get there?"

He heard a sharp exhalation. Sheer relief. "Yeah. But hurry, okay?"

The line went dead before Tony could reply.

He was pulling on his pants when Holt came out of the bathroom. The guy was already fully dressed except for his shoes.

"Sounds like Deputy Doyle is making a move," Holt said as he sat down on the edge of the bed, took a holstered handgun out of his overnighter and calmly began checking it over.

"Uh…yeah," said Tony. "Do you think it's a good idea to take on the entire sheriff's department? I don't see how we're going to be able to do my buddy's sister much good if we're sitting in jail."

Holt glanced at him, eyes glittering in the dim light. "This is just in case. I believe in being prepared."

"Yeah, okay," said Tony, "but here's the thing. Way I see it, the only person who can stop those deputies is a higher authority. Since we don't know how deep into the department this—whatever it is—goes, or how high, that means a judge. The only person a judge is going to listen to, especially this early in the morning, is a lawyer— Brooke's lawyer, in particular. She told me his name is Henderson, and he's in Austin. That's all I know."

"Should be enough." Holt rose, tucked the handgun back in its holster and buckled the holster around his waist so the gun nestled snugly in the small of his back. "I'll see what I can do," he said as he shrugged into his jacket. "Meanwhile, see what you can do to stall 'em. Be careful, though—I think those guys are dangerous."

He paused to shoot Tony a look. "Any idea what you're going to do out there?"

"Me?" Tony let out a breath and reached for his cap and car keys. "I'm gonna try not to think of Custer's Last Stand."

"Wait—didn't the Indians win that one?"

"Yeah," said Tony grimly, "but it was Custer who was outnumbered."

## Chapter 6

"What the hell's the kid doing? How long does it take to find a damn rope?"

"I told you to let me go," Brooke said tightly. "He doesn't know where it is." She had her arms folded across herself to keep her inner shakes from leaking into her voice. Anger or fear? She couldn't be sure. All she did know was that somehow Lonnie's nervous fidgeting made him seem bigger than he was. And definitely more dangerous.

Lonnie gave her a look, that arrogant sneer, which was one of the reasons she disliked him so much. In this case it said louder than words, "I don't trust you out of my sight, lady, not after you killed my best buddy in cold blood."

She didn't know whether he'd have actually voiced the sentiment out loud, because at that moment she saw Daniel emerge from the barn and start toward them, head down, dragging his feet. Her relief was short-lived when she saw what he had slung over one shoulder: not the rope Lonnie'd sent him for, but Lady's old collar and the leash they'd used to take her out around the ranch before she'd gotten too big for both the leash and the house.

"Oh, honey," she said when he came shuffling up in the boneless way that meant he really didn't want to be there at all. "That's way too small for her now. You know that."

He shot her a look she couldn't read, but before he could say a word, Lonnie snatched the leash and collar out of his hands and snarled, "What the hell's the matter with you? I told you to bring a *rope*, not a damn dog leash."

Fear and adrenaline shot through Brooke's body, and she braced herself to step between her child and whatever violence Lonnie might have in mind. But Daniel wasn't about to be intimidated. Sadly, she knew that in his young life, her son had had to deal with a lot worse than a puffed-up bully like Lonnie Doyle.

In spite of her fear, she couldn't help but feel a glow of pride as she watched Daniel step up to the deputy without flinching, face flushed with anger. "What good's a rope gonna do? Don't you know anything? You can't rope a cougar, she's not a *calf,* you know."

Lonnie's face darkened. "You back-talkin' me, boy? You watch your mouth. You understand me?" He moved closer to Daniel, and with her heart pounding, now Brooke *did* step in front of her son.

And the other deputy, Al Hernandez, was there, laying a restraining hand on Lonnie's arm. "Hey, man, what're you doing? The kid's right. No way we're getting a rope on that cat. What we need is a tranq gun."

Lonnie's eyes shifted quickly from Daniel and Brooke to Al and back again in a way that reminded her of something, she couldn't think what, not then.

"I used to have one," she said evenly, ignoring Lonnie. "Unfortunately, somebody took it."

Lonnie swore explosively. "Well, great—that's just great." He shook off Al's hand and went stomping off to confer with the other two deputies, who were lounging against their patrol vehicle, arms and ankles crossed, dark shades on and hats tilted against the rising Texas sun. With a look of what almost seemed like apology, Al went to join them.

As soon as the men were out of earshot, Brooke felt Daniel tugging at her shirtsleeve. She turned on him, saying in a furious whisper, "What were you *thinking?* Are you trying—"

"Mom—Mom—no, wait." He was making frantic shushing gestures, darting sideways looks toward the knot of deputies. "We have to stall for time. That's what I was trying to do. We have to stall them, Mom."

"Daniel? What do you mean, stall? Why? What did you do?"

Flushed and breathless, he put his hand in his pocket and pulled it out just far enough so she could see the shine of metal. His cell phone.

She sucked in a breath and cast the same nervous glance toward the gathering of deputies. "You called someone? *Who?*" For the life of her, she couldn't think of anyone who could help her. Nobody who could stand up to Lonnie and his buddies, anyway.

"Tony," Daniel said, biting his lips to contain his excitement. "He's coming. He said to sit tight, and he'll be right here."

She didn't know whether to laugh or cry. The idea of Tony facing down four armed bullies with badges was ludicrous. She hadn't known him long, but one thing she'd come to understand in that brief time was that in spite of his tough-guy appearance, Tony Whitehall was a very gentle man. But the hope in her son's eyes made her heart ache, and suddenly she was angry—angry with the circumstances, and with Tony, for inciting a fatherless boy to futile hero worship.

"Honey—" her voice shook, and she fought to control it "—Tony's a photographer. What's he going to do against four deputies?"

"I don't know." Daniel folded his arms, and his chin had a stubborn tilt that reminded her—with a surprising pang—of his father. "But he'll help us. I know he will."

"Oh, Daniel…"

At that moment, Lonnie came swaggering back to them, thumbs hooked in his belt, hat tipped back. His bullying stance. He planted himself in front of Brooke but looked down at Daniel as he spoke. *Probably to make himself feel even bigger*, Brooke thought.

"Okay, here's what's gonna happen. You two tell me that lion's such a big pussycat, so what you're gonna do is you're gonna go in there and get that cat into its cage. You understand me?"

"We won't do it!" Daniel yelled before Brooke could reach for him and get a hand over his mouth to shut him up.

Lonnie gave a snort of laughter and looked at his buddies, who were all suddenly looking at the ground, the trees, anywhere but at Lonnie, Brooke or Daniel. "Well, okay, let me tell you what's gonna happen if you don't. If you don't get that cat into that cage, we're gonna shoot it. How's that?"

Daniel gave a gasp of pure outrage. "You can't!"

Lonnie leaned over until his face was on a level with Daniel's, showing his teeth in a mirthless smile. "You wanna bet? The lion attacked. We had no choice but to shoot it, to save your lives."

"That's a lie," said Daniel in a trembling voice, and Brooke pulled him against her side. His body was hot and sweaty; she wondered how she could feel so cold.

"The word of four officers of the law says otherwise," Lonnie said with a shrug, rocking back on his heels. Again, he looked at the other deputies, and in his self-confident smile and their obvious discomfiture, Brooke suddenly saw the truth.

*Daniel's right—they're going to kill Lady. No matter what happens, regardless of what Daniel and I do, they're going to shoot her down and claim it was to save us from being attacked.*

*It's always the same. Something terrible, something awful is going to happen to me. And I can't do anything to stop it.*

*I—a woman—am powerless.*

"Well, looks like I got here just in time."

Brooke gave a violent start as Daniel jerked away from her with a glad cry. "Tony!"

She clamped a hand over her mouth, smothering a small whimpering sound that might have been relief or fear. Somewhere inside her were ringing bells and joyful songs to equal anything of Daniel's, and that in itself was a fearful thing. But drowning out the unexpected gladness she felt at the sight of the man strolling toward them, laden down with his usual array of cameras and bags, was the doubt…the fear. The question, what can he possibly do against four armed deputy sheriffs?

Lonnie had moved to intercept him, one hand held up like a cop stopping traffic. "Hey—where do you think you're going? You got no business here."

"This is going to make a helluva story on tonight's news," Tony said, ignoring him, and although he had several cameras draped over his shoulders and around his neck, he was looking down at the small object he held in one hand. A cell phone. And as he was rapidly stabbing buttons on it with his thumb, he glanced up to add a gleeful, "Terrific follow-up to the story about the killer cat. News flash—Deputies Shoot Pet Cougar in Cold Blood!"

"Hey! You ain't bringing those cameras in here." Lonnie's face was flushed dark with anger. "You hear me? You take one more step and I'm gonna take 'em offa you myself."

Tony smiled. It was his sweet, face-transforming smile, and Brooke, watching, felt something crack and shift inside her. It felt oddly like ice melting.

"Hey," Tony said in his easygoing way, "you're

welcome to 'em. You should probably know, though, that if you damage anything, I'll be filing a lawsuit against the department, the town and the whole damn county the minute the courthouse opens up this morning. And see—" he squinted his eyes and shrugged his broad shoulders "—the thing is, it won't matter, anyway, because I just sent a video of that interesting threat you made to Mrs. Grant and her son here, to my editor's computer." He held up the cell phone and gazed at it with apparent awe. "Amazing what you can do with a cell phone nowadays."

"Cool…" said Daniel on a gleeful exhalation.

Brooke sucked in a breath as Lonnie made a growling sound and took a threatening step toward Tony.

Once again, Al Hernandez interceded. "Come on, man. Don't make it worse," he said to Lonnie as he stepped between the two men. He held up a placating hand to Tony. "Look, all we want to do is take the cougar into custody until the hearing. That's all, okay? Just like we'd do if there was a dog that bit somebody. It's a matter of public safety. The only reason we didn't do it before now is because we didn't have the facilities to hold a dangerous animal like that lion."

"And now you do?" Tony looked and sounded like an interested news reporter. "Mind telling me what arrangements have been made, then, for the animal's safety?"

Lonnie snorted and turned away, his face a study in fury and frustration. Al was staring nervously at the cell phone in Tony's hand. "Ah…well, we, uh…"

"Yeah," Tony said softly, "that's what I thought."

At that moment, the cell phone in his hand began to

play the opening notes of "The William Tell Overture." A smile broke over his tough-guy features, and to Brooke, it seemed like the sun breaking free of clouds. He thumbed the phone on and said, "Whitehall." He listened, and his expression grew somber. "Yes, sir, he certainly is." He held the phone out to Lonnie. "Deputy Doyle? It's for you."

Lonnie took the phone and held it about the way he would have if it had been full of live killer bees. He lifted it to his ear, and there was at least an attempt at bravado, with his deep and abrupt, "Yeah. This is Deputy Sheriff Lonnie Doyle—whom I speakin' to?" Then, looking like he'd been whacked upside the head with a shovel, he spoke in a considerably higher and thinner tone as he pivoted, turning his back on his fascinated audience. "Yessir. Uh…no, sir. No, sir. Yessir, I do understand…."

Brooke felt something warm and solid come to fill the empty space next to her and realized it was Tony. Realized, too, that she still had one hand clamped hard across her mouth. She took it away and looked at him and gave a shivery laugh. "Who—"

"Sshh…" he said, with a slight warning shake of his head, not looking at her but somehow managing to make her feel cloaked in warmth and safety just by being there.

Swallowing her questions and holding inside herself a new sense of wonder, she watched Lonnie take the phone away from his ear. When he turned, his teeth were bared, his face a mask of rage. He looked as though he would have liked to hurl the offending cell phone at the three of them, but once again, it was Al Hernandez who interceded, taking the object from him and handing it back to Tony.

"This ain't over," Lonnie growled, stabbing a finger at Tony, then Brooke. "You hear me? We ain't done, not by a long shot." He stomped over to his sheriff's department SUV, climbed in and slammed the door.

Al threw Brooke a wary glance and went after his partner, getting in on the passenger side. As the SUV bounced back down the lane and through the barn's open breezeway, the other two deputies got into the pickup truck with the cage in the back and followed.

As the sound of the two vehicles faded and a mild morning breeze swirled their dust into eddies, Brooke turned silently and blindly against Tony's broad chest.

He didn't know which surprised him the most: the fact that she'd done it, or that it felt so natural when she did. His arms went around her, and her head came to rest on his shoulder, and her body seemed to fit against his as if they were two broken halves put back together again.

She was trembling in waves, the way someone did when they were crying and trying not to, trying at least not to let anyone else know. He wanted to stroke and comfort her, but the cell phone in his hand was getting in the way. Then somehow it wasn't, as Daniel happily relieved him of it without being asked. And that was another source of wonder to Tony—the fact that not even Daniel seemed to find it odd that a strange man had his arms around his mother.

"Hey," Daniel said, "this isn't a iPhone. It doesn't even have a camera."

Tony let go a gusty breath of laughter. "Okay…busted."

Daniel let out a squawk. "You mean you—"

"Yeah. Sorry. I lied."

Brooke lifted her head to gaze at him with drenched and incredulous eyes. "Dear God—that was a *bluff?*"

"Yeah…" At least, he thought he said something like that. His vision was filled with her eyes, swimming with tears, like sunlight on water, thick lashes clumped together and her mouth all blurred and soft. His senses were overwhelmed with the sweet warmth of her breath and the clean scent of her skin, and the vibrant and graceful curves of her body, nestled against his. It was all he could do not lift his hands to cradle her face and bring it softly…sweetly…gently to his.

Then she was laughing, the back of her hand pressed to her mouth, and he came to himself and reared back with mock outrage. "I'm a professional photojournalist. You think I'd sink so low as to have a camera in my *phone?*"

Her laughter became something that sounded more like a whimper. "Remind me never to play poker with you," she said as she turned to lace her fingers through the fabric of the chain-link fence and rest her forehead on her arm.

"I'm a lousy poker player, actually," Tony said softly, and it took all the will he had not to move close behind her and lay his hands over hers and bury his face in her hair. "A lousy liar, too—normally. I don't know what got into me."

"Well, you did one helluva a job when it counted," she said on a rueful little coda of laughter.

And Daniel crowed, "See? I told you she cusses sometimes."

"Daniel," his mother said in a careful tone, the one mothers everywhere used as their first warning, "don't you think you should go and let Hilda out?"

Tony snapped his fingers. "That's who's missing."

"Yeah," Daniel said, and his face grew dark with anger, "Lonnie made us lock her in the house. He said he'd *shoot* her if she got in his way."

"She's…very protective of us," Brooke said in a low voice as Daniel went running off to the house. "And she really doesn't like Lonnie."

"Interesting," Tony murmured, and he moved up beside her to search the apparently empty compound with narrowed eyes. "Where is she?"

"Hiding. Over there in those rocks. I've never seen her do that before. She senses…" She turned her head to look at him over one braced arm. "Thank you for what you did this morning. You saved Lady's life. I'm sure of it. But—" the muscles in her face flinched, and she finished in a whisper, "—this won't be the end of it. I've never seen Lonnie so mad. He's going to be back."

"He sure does have a hate on for that cougar." He managed to keep his tone light while oily coils of anger were writhing in his belly.

"Oh," Brooke said as she turned, "I'm sure he blames her for Duncan's death."

They walked slowly back toward the house, side by side. "Seems to me," Tony said, "it would make more sense for him to blame you. Since you've been charged with killing him."

"Yeah…" Her forehead furrowed with the little watermark frown as she studied the ground in front of her.

"Doesn't make much sense, does it?" She gave her head a little shake and looked up at him. "You know what else doesn't make sense? How you managed to get hold of a judge and still get over here so fast. It couldn't have been fifteen, maybe twenty minutes after Daniel called you."

"Oh," Tony said. And then he added, "Well," to buy himself time, while nasty little bubbles of guilt burned in his chest like the aftereffects of a bad meal. "I didn't actually get hold of the judge. That would have been your lawyer—what's his name? Mr. Henderson?—he called him."

"Okay…" Brooke said slowly. "But then, you had to call him, didn't you? And you'd have to look up his number, and it couldn't have been easy to reach him, since it was before office hours in the morning…right?"

Memories of childhood flooded him, of being grilled by his mother or sisters after being caught in some misbehavior, and then worse, of being caught in the lies he told to try and save himself. The fact that the desire he'd felt for this woman still sang through his body made the memories weirdly discomfiting. He ran a hand over his scalp and tried to smile. "Actually…I had help. I've been staying with a friend…in town and, uh…"

"Oh," she said. "I'm sorry—I didn't realize—"

Warmth flooded his chest as he saw her cheeks turn pink with embarrassment and understood the conclusion she'd jumped to. "A guy," he said gently. "His name is Holt Kincaid." And then it was his turn to feel the heat of embarrassment as her eyes widened with new understanding. "No—wait," he added, laughing. "It's not *that* kind of friend. No—he's just… He had business in town, and we ran into each other, and with all the media in town for your, uh— Anyway, there weren't any motel rooms to be had, so we've been sharing. That's all. It's not what…" His words dried up under her steady blue gaze.

"Well," she said, with a wry little smile as she faced forward again, "it would have explained a few things."

A gust of surprised laughter escaped him. "Like what?"

There was a pause, but she didn't look at him. Then she hitched in a breath and said, "Like why someone like you isn't married."

He wanted her to look at him again. He wanted her eyes and mouth facing him across a chasm of inches, not feet. He wanted to be having this peculiar conversation with her in a place with soft light and soft places to sit and soft sweet music playing. But she walked beside him and lifted her face to the morning sun, and he had to content himself with watching it caress her skin and cast golden lights into her hair and with imagining his fingers and lips there instead.

He managed to make a small, nonspecific sound, and before he could think of actual words to follow it with, she said, "So…this Holt is the one who called my lawyer?"

"Uh…yeah," he said, "that's right."

"So…is Holt a reporter, too?" She said it warily, defensively, like someone bracing for a disappointment.

And he, so eager not to give it to her, naturally bungled it completely. "Holt? No, no—not a reporter. Nothing like that."

"What does he do?"

"He's, uh…" For a horrible moment, his mind went blank. And then he said the first thing that came into it— from where he didn't know, "He's a traveling salesman."

She nodded and was silent while he mentally closed his eyes and berated himself for an idiot. Then she threw him that wry little smile and said, "Yeah, I can see why you'd be terrible at poker."

He was saved from having to answer that by the 120 or so pounds of canine joy that came hurtling across the yard just then to launch itself upon them from what seemed like every direction at once. There followed an interlude of complete chaos—Hilda barking and whining, wriggling and leaping; Daniel and Brooke both laughing and scolding and yelling, "Hilda! Stop that!" and "Hilda, get *down!* What's the matter with you?"

Tony wasn't spared the dog's attentions, either. Seemingly carried away by her own exuberance, Hilda gave his face an enthusiastic licking, then appeared to realize she might have overstepped her boundaries and, for a moment, seemed to hesitate, almost in apology. But when he gave her a reassuring hug and ruffled her fur, she responded with renewed fervor, her delight seemingly boundless. Tony hadn't had a dog since he'd left home to go off to college, and the lump all this canine affection brought to his throat took him by surprise.

"I guess she's decided she likes me," he said when the pandemonium had subsided enough to allow speech.

"She's a Great Pyrenees—they're herding dogs, you know," Daniel informed him. "She thinks you're part of her flock now."

"Yeah?" Tony couldn't seem to keep the goofy grin from sprawling across his face. Why did that seem like the greatest accolade he'd received since his Pulitzer?

"Hey, Mom," Daniel yelled. "We didn't have breakfast.

Can we have blueberry pancakes? Tony—did you have breakfast yet? Mom—can Tony eat breakfast with us?"

What could he say?

What could she say? Brooke watched her son go off with the big, tough-looking photojournalist in tow, like a little jaunty tugboat pulling a beat-up barge; and again, she didn't know whether to laugh at the sight or cry.

*Why do I trust this man? How can I trust him? He lied about this…Holt Kincaid guy. And he's right. He's a terrible liar. But why? Why would he lie?*

And she had such a lousy track record, trusting men.

"My mom makes the best blueberry pancakes in the whole world." Daniel drew a forefinger across his plate to scoop up the last of the whipped topping mixed with blueberry juice and popped it in his mouth, then aimed a look of wide-eyed innocence at Tony. "Don't you think?"

"Daniel," Brooke breathed.

And Tony said obligingly, "Absolutely. The best."

"My mom's a really good cook," said Daniel, slyly avoiding Tony's eyes.

Brooke rolled her eyes. "Oh, brother. Come on, kiddo. Crisis time is over. This isn't a holiday, so if you're finished stuffing yourself, go get yourself ready for school."

"Aw, Mom…"

"Daniel…"

"But I'm not missing anything important, Mom, I don't have any tests or anything. Honest. I can miss one day. Mrs. Hackley won't care. I know she won't."

Brooke leaned against the sink, arms folded, pancake

turner in one hand, and regarded her son. *My protector*. Because she knew that was what was on his mind. He was afraid to go off and leave her alone. Afraid Lonnie might come back. The thought of Daniel facing down Lonnie made her go cold all over. "Daniel," she said softly, "I'll be all right. He's not going to come back. Not today."

Her son stared at her, holding her gaze with his eyes fierce and dark, and she wondered if he was remembering, as she was, all the times she'd held him or sat beside his bed and soothed him with those words. *Oh, Daniel, I hope not....*

"I can stay," Tony said. Brooke jerked and looked at him, and so did Daniel. Tony shrugged and shifted half around in his chair so he was facing her, although it was to Daniel he spoke when he added, "Just in case your mom needs help. How would that be?"

Daniel considered for a moment, then nodded judiciously. "Okay. I guess that would work." He slipped off his chair and crossed the kitchen at a mature and dignified walk. Until he reached the doorway. Then he took off like a shot.

Brooke gave a little squeak of laughter, closed her eyes and put her hand over her mouth. She waited until she heard Daniel's bedroom door slam, then looked at Tony and said, "Thank you."

"No problem." His eyes had a warm glow. *Like honey*, she thought. Not lion eyes, not this time. "He's worried about you," he said softly, tilting his head in the direction Daniel had gone.

"He's always been like that." She sighed and turned

to drop the pancake turner in the sink. "He's very protective of me. I think he gets it from his father."

Behind her, Tony made a sound, incredulous and disbelieving. "How is that? The man was protective of you, so much so that he bought you a giant dog and a tranquilizer gun, and then he *beat* you?"

She stood still, eyes closed, gripping the edge of the sink, fighting for control. Then she turned and said carefully, "It's not that unusual, actually. Or contradictory. It's probably two sides of the same coin." Tony shook his head and looked away, squinting as if the sight of her had become painful.

She went to sit in the chair Daniel had left vacant and leaned toward him, hands clasped on the tabletop. "I know you don't understand." *Oh, and I want you to. Why is that, I wonder?* "But the fact that Duncan was protective of me was one of the things that attracted me to him in the first place. I *needed* that."

"Protective is one thing. Abusive is another." Tony's eyes were hard and glittery, and his face had a set, bunched look that reminded her of a pit bull.

"Yes," Brooke said gently. "But sometimes they go together. It was all part of him thinking of me as his possession, I suppose, but at the time, I loved the attention, and the way he fussed over me. I was—" She sat back abruptly and cleared her throat. "You probably don't want to hear this."

"Yeah, I do." It was a low growl, and that reminded her of a pit bull, too.

"Okay, then." She lifted her head and faced him defiantly. "I hadn't ever had that kind of attention—not from a man. My father was…indifferent, I guess, is the closest I can come to it. You see…I was adopted. There were two of us. I have a sister, a twin. Fraternal, although we're nothing at all alike. My parents had a natural son—Cody. He was about ten years older than my sister and me."

She paused, and Tony said, "Was?"

She nodded. Having tested herself and having felt nothing, she was glad to know the walls she'd built around that part of her life were still holding fast. "Yes. He died in the same car accident that killed my parents. I don't think my dad ever wanted to adopt in the first place. He was happy with his only son. But he agreed to it to make my mom happy, because she wanted a little girl. He was never cruel to us or anything like that. He was just…distant. I don't think he could help it, really, but at the time I thought there was something wrong with me, that it was my fault he didn't love me. Or my sister. So I didn't have a lot of confidence when it came to boys, you know?"

*Oh, God, do I sound pitiful? I don't want to! I'm not!*

She wanted to tell him that. Tell him she wasn't that needy creature anymore, that she didn't need anyone protecting her, that she was capable of protecting herself. Why, she didn't know, but it suddenly seemed so important that he know—and maybe even more important that *she* know—she wasn't that person and wasn't making the same mistake all over again.

*Oh, God, I'm not…am I? Am I drawn to this man because he makes me feel safe?*

There were things she wanted to say to him…ask

him. But he sat so silently, his big body still as stone, looking at her with eyes that weren't soft any longer but burning like fire. Lion's eyes again. A strange shivering awareness poured through her body, rolling over her just beneath her skin, raising goose bumps and tightening her breasts until her nipples hurt. It was scary and at the same time exciting, and she didn't know how long it might have lasted or how it might have ended, because Daniel came dashing back into the kitchen, with his backpack slung over his shoulder, and just like that the spell was broken.

"Mom, you have to take me to school, because I missed the bus," said Daniel, stating the obvious.

Tony shoved back his chair and stood up. "I left in kind of a hurry this morning. I'm going to need to go pick up some stuff at the motel, so I can drop him at school, if you want."

"Cool," said Daniel. Then, remembering, he added, "Mom? Are you gonna be okay?"

"I'll be fine," she assured him, and Tony added his assurances that he'd be right back.

Brooke stood on the back porch steps, hugging herself, and watched her son get into a car with a man she'd known all of a few days. And again, she asked herself, *Why do I trust this man?*

And then, *Do I trust this man?*

Something was bothering her, an uneasiness that hadn't been there before. *What is it? Something's not right. But I can't think what it is!*

She gave Hilda's head an absentminded pat and went back into the kitchen. And it was while she was clearing away the last of breakfast from the table, and replaying that strangely intense conversation with Tony in her mind, that it came to her.

He didn't ask.

All her life, whenever anyone learned she was adopted, and that she had a twin sister, they always, *always* asked questions, showed curiosity. At the very least, interest.

Tony was a naturally curious person, in addition to being a journalist. He asked questions about everything. Was curious about everything. Interested in everything.

But he hadn't asked a single question when she'd told him she was adopted. That she had a twin. He hadn't shown any sign of curiosity or interest in knowing more about it.

How odd, she thought. It's almost as if he already knew.

## Chapter 7

Walking into the motel room he'd been sharing with Holt for the past several days, Tony experienced what he thought of as a reverse epiphany—not a burst of light and knowledge, but an enveloping shroud of shadowy self-doubt.

What was he thinking? Just because his belly was full of the best blueberry pancakes he'd ever eaten in his life, his ego pumped up with the hero worship of a fatherless boy, and his libido in a state of itchy alert brought on by the unexpected embrace of the most beautiful woman he'd met in a long, long time, that was no excuse for completely losing his functioning mind.

"What are we doing?" he said to Holt, who was bent over his laptop, peering intently at the screen. "Why are we trusting this woman? Okay, I know we decided to proceed on the assumption she did not kill her ex. But what if we're wrong and all the evidence that says she did is right?"

Holt glanced up at him and said mildly, "Afraid you're losing your perspective?"

Tony snorted. "Like I ever had any. I told you at the beginning, she's my best friend's long-lost baby sister, I *want* her to be innocent. Then there's the fact that I've never seen a more beautiful woman in my life. And I'm a photographer, man—I mean, I've seen some beautiful woman, you know?"

Holt's smile was sardonic. "Come on."

"That's right, I forgot. You've never seen her." He picked up the camera he'd been doing most of his shooting with and popped out the flash card. From the front pocket of his accessory case, he took a card reader, inserted the card and handed the whole thing to Holt. "Here—that thing's got a USB port, right? Plug this in. Maybe you'll see what I'm dealing with."

Holt took the card reader with a shrug and plugged it into his laptop, and a few moments later both men watched in silence—a silence that bordered on reverence—as a slide show of images flashed across the computer screen. Presently, Holt cleared his throat and said, "Okay. Just because she's..."

"Gorgeous..."

"Okay, that works—gorgeous, yeah. That doesn't make her an evil person."

"What? I never said that."

"Then why," Holt said blandly, "are you holding it against her?"

"What? I'm not. That's just…"

Holt ejected the card and reader and handed it back to him. "Look, you've been out there every day for the past…what? Three days? Spending time with the lady. You haven't had these doubts about her before, so… what's up? What's changed?"

"Nothing," said Tony, with all the conviction of a kid standing in front of a broken window with a slingshot in his pocket.

Holt gave him a narrow look, then grinned. "Ah—I see. Getting a little too close for comfort, are we? Looking for a reason to bail out while you still can?"

"No! What are you talking about? Nothing of the kind, man. She's my buddy's baby sister, she's in a jam, and I'm trying to help her out—that's all. End of story." He paused, then added, with an uncomfortable shrug, "Anything else would be creepy."

"Yeah, yeah…" Holt was on his feet, shrugging into a leather jacket. "Having been a commitment-phobe all my life, believe me, I know one when I see one. Anyway—beside the point. It's not just a matter of taking Brooke Grant on faith. We know there's something off about those deputies, Doyle in particular. If this were a court of law and we were the jury, we'd have all kinds of grounds for reasonable doubt. You ask me, I think the kid's got reason to be worried, and I think it's a good idea you plan on staying out there with them for the time being."

"You know something I don't?" Tony asked, going still inside.

Holt nodded, looking grim as he pocketed his wallet

and tucked his weapon into its holster in the small of his back. "Finally got hold of Sam. She contacted a friend in DEA. Seems they, in cooperation with ICE, have been looking at our local sheriff's department for a while now." He reached for the doorknob, then turned. "I'm heading into Austin now to talk with the agents. I don't know what, if anything, this has to do with the murder of Duncan Grant, but you watch your back, understand?" He went out, muttering under his breath.

"You betcha," Tony said to the closing door. He wasn't absolutely certain, but what it sounded like the detective had said there at the last was, "Just what I need…get my clients' best friend killed…"

He hauled in a breath to quiet his accelerating pulse and began to pack.

Driving back to Brooke's, he tried to direct his thoughts toward the ramifications of a whole sheriff's department engaged in corruption and illegal activities of various kinds, and what that might mean as far as Brooke's and Daniel's—and his own—personal safety was concerned. But, like a badly trained horse, his mind kept wanting to go somewhere else.

*Commitment-phobe? Me?*

*Ridiculous,* he told himself. *This woman is my best friend's baby sister, and she's in trouble. Taking advantage of her would be unforgivable.*

And his mind whispered in Brooke's voice, *It would have explained…why someone like you isn't married.*

*Look,* he told himself, *I have perfectly good reasons for avoiding permanence in relationships, number one being a job that takes me to the far corners of the earth most of the time.*

And his mind replied, You grew up mostly without a dad for the same reason, didn't you?

*Yes,* he told himself, through mentally clenched teeth, *but that doesn't make me a commitment-phobe. I intend to settle down someday…at the right time…with the right person. I* will.

Lost in the dismal swamp of his thoughts, he almost missed the turnoff to Brooke's driveway. Did miss it, in fact, and had to back up a few yards to make the turn. As he was doing that, he noticed a man working with a horse in the pasture across the road. The man was wearing jeans and a blue work shirt and a straw cowboy hat, and looked Hispanic. Being the son of a cowboy, and with some considerable experience with horses himself, Tony paused to watch the man in action. He was admiring the trainer's skill and patience when the fellow looked up and noticed he had an audience. Tony nodded and waved. The horse trainer quickly ducked his head to hide his face and turned away. Coiling his rope to make a short lead, he led the mare at a brisk trot back toward the barn and corrals, which were just visible on the other side of a stand of live oaks.

*Huh,* Tony thought as he turned into Brooke's lane. *Friendly fellow.*

Brooke came out to meet him when he parked in what had become his usual spot, beside her pickup truck. She looked flushed and eager, as if she'd been waiting for him. Watching for him.

Inside his chest he felt a little tremor of gladness at the thought. Gladness…and some unease.

"Everything okay?" he asked her.

She nodded. "Daniel...?"

"Made it to school just fine."

Then, for a moment, there was silence while they looked at each other, and there was a new awkwardness, which hadn't been there the other times he'd come, loaded down with his cameras, to spend the day taking pictures of the cougar. This was no longer about the cougar, and they both knew it. Somewhere, somehow, when he wasn't paying attention, a line had been crossed. Just what kind of line and what it meant, he didn't know.

"Uh, hey," he said, clutching at something to fill the awkward moment, "I was just watching your neighbor over there across the road. Has some nice horses."

"Oh, yeah, that's Rocky." She poked the tips of her fingers into the back pockets of her jeans and hitched one shoulder. "The Mirandas—they're great. They help me out sometimes—a lot, actually."

"Huh," said Tony. "Must be me, then. He practically ran off when I waved."

She smiled and made a little gesture as if to hide it— a kind of shyness he'd glimpsed in her a time or two before. "Oh, that was probably one of their, um, cousins."

"Cousins?"

"Yeah. Rocky and Isabel have a lot of, uh, cousins. They come and work for them sometimes...you know?" He stared at her blankly, and she gave him a sideways look of exasperation. "Oh, for heaven's sake. *Illegals,* Tony. He probably thought you were INS, or ICE—

whatever they call themselves now. Poor guy—he's probably packing to leave as we speak. Well, I'll call Isabel…tell her you're harmless."

*Are you harmless, Tony? Why is it I doubt you when you're out of my sight, and the minute I see you, I'm right back there, trusting you again?*

*Now, when I've got no business trusting anyone, much less a man who looks like a gang enforcer.*

Feeling awkward suddenly, needing something to do with her hands, she opened the backseat passenger-side door and peered in. On the other side of the car, Tony was gathering up various camera and equipment bags, leaving a small duffel bag on the seat. "Do you want this, too?" she asked, picking it up.

"Yeah—here. Give me that." He took the duffel bag from her, then held it, hefted it and looked at her in a way that made her wonder suddenly if he felt as awkward about this as she did. The idea made her want to smile, with a strange shivery excitement that made her think of her twelve-year-old self passing notes to Tommy Hanson in English class.

"I hope you don't mind," he said. "I thought it would be best if I stayed…you know, for a while. If you don't have a spare room, I can sleep on the couch."

"Oh. Well, are you sure? That's… Thank you." The shivery feeling expanded inside her, and her heart began to beat faster. She folded her arms across her chest and laughed a little as she turned to walk beside him. "You don't have to sleep on the couch, though. I've got a spare room, if you don't mind the mess." Glancing down at the duffel bag, she said, "Is that all you've got? No suitcase?"

He gave a wry puff of laughter. "Nope—that's it. I came kind of on the spur of the moment."

"Well then…" She paused to look over at him. "You must be about out of clean clothes. If you have any laundry, I'd be glad to—"

Having preceded her up the back porch steps, he opened the door for her, even though he was the one loaded down with bags. And smiled down at her as she came up the steps after him. "Okay, I wouldn't mind the use of your washing machine, but I'm capable of doing my own laundry."

"But I don't mind, really—" She was facing him on the top step, crowded close to him while he held the door for her to slip through. She should have felt claustrophobic, being so close to such a big man, one she barely knew. But his eyes had that mellow honey glow, and the distance between them seemed…not too narrow, but too wide.

"Brooke," he said softly, in a voice that reminded her of the mountain lion's purr, and her vision grew shimmery around the edges. "We're letting the flies in."

"Oh." Unnerved, she moved past him, onto the screened porch. He followed her, letting the door slam shut, and she watched the way the muscles bunched in his arms and back as he lifted the duffel bag onto the washing machine. She hoped he hadn't noticed her schoolgirlish lapse, prayed that that revealing moment at the top of the steps had somehow slipped past him.

He turned back to her, shifting the bags hanging by their straps from various parts of his body. "I do *not* expect you to wash my clothes." And he was smiling that incongruously sweet, heart-melting smile. "See, I was raised by a mom, along with seven sisters, not one of whom believed they were put on this earth to wait on a man."

She let go a laugh, which emerged sounding light and casual; only she would know it was rooted in desperation. "Wow, tell me again why it is you aren't married?"

"Funny," he said as his smile slipped awry. "My sisters keep asking me the same thing."

*What is it with everybody lately?* Tony thought as he followed Brooke down the hallway to what really was more of a "spare" than a "guest" room, being cluttered with all the usual things there was simply no other place for—sewing machine and ironing board and books and a boy's outgrown toys. Suddenly everyone he knew seemed to be interested in his marital status. And, frankly, it was beginning to irritate him. Holt calling him a commitment-phobe…his sisters pointing out to him the fact that he was the last unmarried holdout in the family… What should it matter to them, anyhow? It wasn't as if his mom was desperate for grandkids—she had so many now, he didn't know how she kept track of them all. A couple of his oldest brothers and sisters even had grandkids, for God's sake!

He'd chosen a career that wasn't conducive to hearth, home and rug rats, that was all. What was he supposed to do? Give up his livelihood? Find a new one? The hell with *that!*

He dumped his cameras on the double bed that occupied a good bit of the available space in the small room and stood for a moment, frowning at nothing as a memory came crowding into his mind. A memory from a few years back, a time when he'd come close to losing everything—including his best friends and his own life.

*Cory...and he's had more beer than he usually drinks, and he's leaning in toward me, across the table in a restaurant in the Philippines, and I can hear him saying, "...I'm thinking maybe it's time to be settling down, cut down on the travel, have some kids before I'm too old to enjoy 'em."*

*And me, nodding my head like I know all the answers and saying, "You've got the old nesting urge. Happens. Hasn't happened to me yet, but I've heard about it."*

And he thought about Sam, and how she had thought she couldn't have her career and Cory both, and had almost lost everything by waiting too long. And now look at the two of them—happily married and both still off to the far corners, doing their thing....

*No kids yet, though. Kids make all the difference. Kids need their parents around while they're growing up. Both of 'em, preferably.*

He still had a few things to bring in from the car—his computer, mainly. He went down the hall and through the kitchen, and was struck by how quiet it seemed—and how empty—without Brooke. It had been all of five minutes since she'd left him in the spare room and had gone out to take care of some chore or other. And already he missed her.

And what the hell was *that?*

He went outside, telling himself he was just going to get his laptop, that he wasn't going to go looking for Brooke, who had her own business to attend to, after all, and didn't need him tagging along, getting in her way. He'd gotten as far as unlocking the trunk when he looked up and saw three people walking up the lane. One of them was the horse trainer he'd been watching earlier, and he was accompanied by a Hispanic couple, who Tony assumed must be the nice neighbors, Rocky and Isabel.

Intrigued, especially after what Brooke had told him about the nature of the neighbors' "cousins," Tony looped the strap of his laptop carrier over his shoulder, closed the trunk and waited.

The trio had reached the yard when Hilda came bounding out of the barn to greet them, with her whole body wagging, along with her tail. Obviously, the neighbors were on her favorites list. Brooke followed a moment later, and she and the woman—pretty, and shorter and plumper than Brooke but probably about the same age—exchanged hugs. The woman's husband spoke to Brooke, gesturing from time to time toward his "cousin," who stood by with his hat in his hands, looking exceedingly uneasy. Tony had already started to amble toward them, in what he hoped was a non-threatening manner, when Brooke's head jerked toward him, and the look on her face made him quicken his step and his pulse kick into high gear.

"What is it?" he asked in a low voice as he moved close beside her. "Something wrong?"

She opened her mouth, but before she could say anything, Tony said, "Hi, I'm Tony," nodded at the woman and leaned forward to offer his hand, first to her husband, then to his cousin. The cousin hesitated, then shook his hand, bobbed his head and mumbled something in Spanish, while Brooke made hurried introductions.

"Rocky and Isabel—my neighbors. This is Tony. He's, uh…"

"You are her friend," Rocky said. "We have seen you here. That is why when my cousin told me what he saw, I told him he should tell you."

Tony nodded but didn't prompt him. His senses felt honed, razor sharp, and he had in his mind an image of a cougar watching a fawn…eyes like lasers, body gone still and taut, only the tip of her tail twitching….

Beside him he felt a tremor run through Brooke, like a fine electrical current. He wanted to put his arm around her and nestle her against his side. Wanted to so badly, he folded his arms to keep himself from doing it.

"Tell him," Brooke said in a rasping voice.

Rocky nodded and glanced at his cousin, who looked at the ground. "The day Duncan—Mr. Grant—was killed, my cousin, he was working there—" he made a sweeping gesture with his arm "—with the horses. He saw a sheriff's car—one of the four-wheel-drive ones— drive out of the lane over there, the one nobody uses."

"Where Duncan's car was found." Brooke's voice was barely audible. She cleared her throat, and Rocky went on.

"*Sí*—yes. And that was also a sheriff's SUV. But that is not the one that drove away."

"You're saying," said Tony slowly, "there were *two* sheriff's vehicles here that day?" His heart knocked hard against his breastbone.

Rocky nodded. "*Sí*—yes. That's right. And one drove away. My cousin didn't say anything at first, because he didn't want any trouble with the police, you know?" He glanced at his cousin, who continued to stare steadfastly at the ground. "And when he told me, I didn't want to say anything, because I was afraid for *her*." He tipped his head toward Brooke, but he spoke to Tony, in a low and intense voice. "She was alone, you know? I didn't know what they might do. But now that you are here…" It was his wife he looked at now, and she stepped up beside him and he slipped his arm around her waist.

"You can do something," said Isabel fervently, and her dark eyes glistened with appeal. "Maybe?"

It was late that evening before Tony managed to pass the news along to Holt. He'd been leaving messages on the detective's voice mail all day, and finally got a call back around ten, while he was in his room, folding his freshly washed underwear.

"Sorry—I've been in conference with members of various federal law-enforcement agencies all day. What's up?"

Tony told him. "As far as I'm concerned," he concluded, "this cinches it. One of Grant's fellow deputies killed him. Most likely Lonnie."

"Only one problem. A little thing called motive."

Tony let out an explosive breath. "I was hoping you'd come up with something on your end."

"Wish I could say I had. The feds are investigating the Colton County Sheriff's Department, along with several others in reasonable proximity to the border, on suspicion of trafficking in drugs and illegals. All they'll tell me is it's an ongoing investigation, and they don't want anybody coming in and messing up their case until they're ready to make their move. They did say both Duncan Grant and Lonnie Doyle are—or in Grant's case, were—quote, 'persons of interest.'"

"Okay, so…a falling-out between partners in crime? That doesn't seem much of a stretch, given these two were always going at each other anyway."

"True. But why do it like that—with a tranquilizer gun and a mountain lion? At the guy's ex-wife's place? *That's* what doesn't make any sense."

"And now Lonnie Doyle wants the lion dead. That doesn't make sense, either. It's not like she's an eyewitness, not one that could testify against him, anyway."

On the other end of the line, there was a soft hissing sound—an exhalation. "The key to this whole thing," Holt said, "is that cat."

After that conversation with Holt, Tony felt too wired to even think about sleep. The house was silent, and in the stillness, those words keep playing over and over in his head: *the key is that cat.*

He opened his door and stepped out into the hallway. Brooke's door, across and a little way down from his, was closed. Daniel's was open a couple of inches—for the light, Tony imagined, remembering how he'd liked to leave his door open when he was a kid, because there was just enough light from the one left burning on the front porch to dilute the darkness in his room to shadowy grays. Here the light was from the kitchen— Brooke had left one on above the stove. He moved through the kitchen and onto the back porch, treading lightly and opening and closing doors without sound.

Standing on the porch and looking out, he discovered the yard and the landscape beyond bathed in the pewter glow of a rising full moon. He paused there for a moment to appreciate the subtle variations of blue and silver and gray, wishing he'd thought to bring a camera with him, unwilling to make the trip back to his room lest he wake someone, knowing he didn't really have the equipment with him to capture the magical quality of the light, anyway.

Opening the screen door—with only one squeak, though it seemed incredibly loud in the stillness of the night—he went outside and down the steps. And a magnificent beast with a silvery-white coat that seemed to lift and float around her like feathers came romping toward him from the direction of the barn.

"Hey, Hilda," he whispered, offering his hand. "How you doin', girl?"

The dog accepted his hug with a lick and a grin and went dancing back toward the barn, clearly delighted with the night, the moon and his company. Tony didn't know whether he'd intended to go that way, but with the dog as his flagship, her tail floating behind her like a banner in a light wind, how could he not follow?

He went through the deeply shadowed barn, and when he stepped out into the moonlit lane that led down between the animal pens to the cougar's enclosure, he wondered if it had been more than restlessness and the cougar's haunting…more even than moonlight and the dog's guidance…that had brought him to that place.

He'd never thought of himself as a mystical soul, and no doubt the influence of the moonlight had something to do with it, but he found himself thinking of things like…*fate*. And whether there really might be something to the notion that some people…some souls…were simply destined to find each other, no matter the time or place or the odds against it.

Inside the cougar's compound, blurred by the silvery netting of the chain-link fence, he could see the dark and slender form turn when she heard the dog come bounding up…turn, then stand, waiting, alert and still, with one hand resting on the head of the magnificent animal beside her.

His breath stopped; his heartbeat surged. He yearned… grieved…mourned for his cameras, the way only another photographer might understand.

It was, simply, the most breathtakingly beautiful thing he'd ever seen. The stuff of legend and fantasy, woman and lion, motionless in the moonlight, frozen in time and space. They stared at him and he stared back, while memory returned him to that moment on the trail in the High Sierras when he'd come face-to-face with a beast that could have killed him with one swipe of her paw. He'd been afraid then, of course, because he was old enough to know he should be afraid. But mostly what he'd felt was a profound sense of wonder. Of *awe*.

Now, gazing at the woman and the lion in the moonlight, his grown-up self felt the same wonder, the same awe…and the deepest fear, a kind of fear he'd never known before.

He felt stripped and vulnerable, naked and afraid. Because he knew…he *knew* in the depths of his being that his heart wasn't his anymore. That somehow, when he wasn't paying attention, he'd given it away. And in doing so, had given to another human being—to this woman—the power to hurt him as he'd never been hurt before.

All of this—the changing of his life forever—took place in the space of a moment, a few dozen heartbeats, no more. Then the cougar turned on herself in the fluid, boneless way of all felines and went streaking across the compound like a trick of the light, toward the rocky outcropping, flowed up and over it like quicksilver, and was gone.

Brooke came on, and he knew her eyes were locked with his, even though her expression was undecipherable to him, its subtle nuances lost to the moonlight shadows. He waited for her in silence, fingers of one hand woven through the chain-link fabric, those of the other through the silky fur of the dog panting happily beside him. And he understood now why Brooke so often did the same. He waited while she opened the gate and stepped through, then closed it carefully behind her and clicked the padlock into place.

She turned to him, and he would have spoken then. He drew breath to break the silence. And she reached up and touched his face…laid her hand along the side of his face while she looked into his eyes. He saw the moon reflected in the blackness of her eyes just for a moment. Then she swayed upward, just enough, and kissed him.

# Chapter 8

The kiss was light and soft and sweet. He held his breath and closed his eyes because it seemed not quite real, except for the heavy thumping of his heart.

A great stillness came over him. Later, when he thought about it—when he could think again—it seemed to him like the stillness he felt when waiting for an elusive subject to move into the perfect spot, waiting for the exact moment when he would finally capture it. His body was still…but inside, every nerve and sinew and sense vibrated with energy and excitement and that sense of awe and wonder that never seemed to diminish no matter how many times he experienced that moment.

But this was different, of course, and it ended just when he felt his hands begin to lift of their own accord, and he knew he was about to touch her—her arms, first, then…who knows?—against all good sense and his better judgment. It ended when she rocked back on her heels—although she let her hand linger a while longer on his face before it slid down to rest on his chest—and he let his breath go, carefully. She went on gazing at him then, with her head tilted slightly, and her hair, loose, for once, in a carefree fall of subtly curving layers, seemed to lift and float around her face like feathers.

"Are you absolutely sure you're not gay?" Her voice was a rusty sound, and he responded with a feeble noise, which he, with his manly self-image, would not accept—could not possibly believe—was a whimper.

"Positive," he managed, more croak than voice, and tried to laugh.

"Hmm…well." Her hand moved slightly on his chest, drifting more than stroking, and where it paused again, he felt the heat of his body soak through his shirt and merge with hers. "Just so you know—" she hitched in a breath "—I only act like a brazen hussy during the full moon, so you'd better take advantage of the opportunity while you can." And he heard a new note in her voice, one he had no trouble recognizing, though she'd tried her best to hide it under a camouflage of sultry laughter.

"And…that's the problem," he said gently, on firmer ground now that he understood how vulnerable, how uncertain she was. "I would be."

"Oh." Her hand stilled…curled on his chest, and from only that contact, he felt the fine tremors coursing through her. "I see—you'd be taking advantage of me in my present desperate circumstances." Her chin came up, and her hair slithered back over her shoulders. He could see her lips curve in a smile that even the metallic colors of moonlight couldn't rob of softness and warmth. "Tony," she said in a husky whisper, "you are a very sweet man."

He gave a spurt of laughter. "Oh, thanks—just what every manly man wants to he—"

"Stop." Her fingertips, laid warm against his lips, caught the last word. "You have no idea how appealing that quality is to me."

"And you…have no idea how appealing you are…to me." He felt her arms, the skin cool but warming rapidly under his palms, and wondered when his body had given itself permission to touch her.

"Then why…"

"Don't I want to kiss you? Because I know if I do, I won't want to stop." And why do my hands insist on slipping up to your shoulders? *And…is this your neck I feel, so warm and vibrant, your pulse racing like a wild thing against my palms?*

"Well, darlin'—" and the pure Texas in her voice made him smile "—nobody's askin' you to."

"Brooke…" His heartbeat was thunder, not fast but slow.…

"Hush up." She swayed toward him. "Let's just cross that bridge when we come to it, okay? For now, why don't you try it, and if neither one of us wants to stop, we'll just keep on doin' it—how's that?"

*I am a brazen hussy*, she thought. When did this happen?

She didn't care. All she wanted—and she wanted it

with a desperation that astounded her—was for him to kiss her again. *Not again—I kissed him the first time. That doesn't count. Tony…kiss me…please…because if you don't, I think I will die of embarrassment, and if it's possible to die of wanting, I will do that, too.*

And then he *was* kissing her, and his hand cradled her head like a newborn babe. She gave a whimper of thankfulness; and her arms went around his big, solid body; and it felt to her like a bulwark, a bastion of safety in the chaos her world had become.

The kiss was sweet and gentle, as she'd expected his kiss would be. What she hadn't expected was that it would be—she was no expert on kissing, but the word *skilled* came to mind. Thorough…sensitive…not overbearing, and yet…utterly devastating. Something shattered inside her, leaving her groundless and trembling. She lost her place in the world; now she clung to him as she would hold on to a tree in a hurricane.

Panic seized her. Her mind cried out to him to stop.

And he did. Gently easing his mouth away from hers with soft caresses, which lingered on her lips like something so delicious…so heavenly that she licked her lips to keep the taste of him with her just a little longer, already knowing she was addicted. Already wanting more.

"Hmm," she murmured, eyes closed, swaying a little. "See, I knew you'd be a good kisser." She heard the slur in her words and knew she sounded drunk…or besotted. And didn't care.

He laughed, and the fact that it sounded shaken rather than smug endeared him to her even more. His arms enveloped her, and she felt small and cared for—a novelty for her, being five-ten in her socks. She tilted her head back so she could look at him, marveling at the rugged landscape of his face in the moonlight, marveling that a man with such a face could be so incredibly tender. And it came to her then, in that moment, that his face was actually…beautiful.

"Why did you stop?" she asked in a whisper.

He tipped his head to look at her, bringing his mouth close to hers again. "I thought you wanted me to."

"I did." She swallowed. Audibly. "Just for a minute. I was…I couldn't—"

"Yeah," he whispered, "me, too."

"I'm okay now, though, I think. Can we do it again?"

"Are you sure?"

"Yes…please…"

This time they broke from the kiss, both of them, breathless and shaky. Tony cradled Brooke's head against his rapidly thumping heart and stared bleakly over her head at the colorless landscape beyond the chain-link fence and wondered how he could have let himself come to this in so short a time.

*She trusts me. Daniel trusts me. Hell, even the dog trusts me. And I've lied to them all. She doesn't know who I really am or why I'm really here. She doesn't even know who she really is. How am I going to tell her?*

*Oh, God…I have to tell her, now.*

"Brooke—" he began, at the same moment she said, "Tony—"

He paused, and they both said together, "There's something I have to tell you—" They both stopped again, laughing in a rueful, pain-filled way.

"Me, first," she said in a thickened voice, pulling back and gazing earnestly at him. The back of one hand was pressed against her nose, and above it her eyes were dark and still, like deep forest ponds, reflecting only the moonlight. It was only because he was holding her that he felt her shiver.

"Okay," he said, "but only if we find a warmer spot first. You're cold." But it was he who felt cold—on the outside where her body had nestled, and inside, deep in the pit of his stomach, where the fear was.

She shook her head but turned in his embrace and slipped an arm around his waist as they began to walk together back toward the barn. "Not cold. Nervous, maybe." She glanced at him, then quickly away, making him realize what an understatement that was.

He wanted to say something to take away her fear, but his own was so deep, he didn't trust himself to utter a sound. He couldn't ask her what she might have to confess, to be nervous about—how could he, when uppermost in his mind was that she was about to tell him she'd killed her husband, after all, and that he'd been wrong about her all along? So he walked beside her in the moonlight, her arm around him and his around her. It occurred to him that they must look like lovers, but while her body felt warm and vital against him, the cold he felt inside was the sick and clammy chill of dread.

In the barn, they sat on a bale of hay in a patch of moonlight framed by the big open door, side by side, like children on a bench. Brooke shifted, turning to half face him as she took one of his hands in both of hers. Her shoulders lifted as she took a breath.

"Brooke," he burst out, unable to stand it anymore, "I can understand if it was self-defense—"

"What?" She blinked and shook her head sharply, as if coming out of a daze. Then clapped a hand to her forehead. "Oh—oh, God. You thought—oh, stupid me." She stared at him for a moment, then smiled crookedly and said, with that Texas twang he was beginning to find so unexpectedly endearing, "Tony, you poor thing. You're sittin' there thinkin' you're about to find out you've just been kissin' a cold-blooded killer, aren't you?"

"Well," he said in a garbled imitation of a frog.

"No, it's my fault, and I'm sorry. I should have thought." She faced forward again and didn't reclaim his hand, bracing hers on the edge of the bale instead as she rocked herself slightly. She gave a faint laugh. "Funny thing is, I never even thought about…that. Can you believe that? I actually forgot for maybe a minute." Her voice took on an edge, and she threw him a quick, intense look over her shoulder. "The answer to the question that's eatin' you up inside is, no, I did not kill my husband. *Ex*-husband," she amended wearily, closing her eyes. "You can believe that or not…but it's true."

Tony cleared his throat and found his voice was functional again, and that the cold place in his belly was fading. "I do believe you. I have been believing you. That's why I'm here."

"But you've had doubts." She looked at him over her shoulder again, sadly this time. "Otherwise, you wouldn't have thought I was about to confess."

He tried to smile. "I can't argue with the logic of that,

so I'm not even going to try. But since we both know you're not a murderer, what is this *thing* you feel you have to tell me?"

She looked at him for a long time, her eyes lingering, not on his eyes, but on his mouth…his shoulders, his chest. The stark hunger…yearning…he saw on her face nearly stopped his heart, then quickened it again. She turned away quickly, but not before he saw her lips quiver…saw her press them tightly together to stop it.

In a voice so low he had to lean closer to hear it, she said, "I want you to know…it felt so good, you holding me. Felt *too* good, you kissing me, me kissing you—I didn't want it to end. But…I thought, before I let this go any further, you should know exactly who you'd be kissing." She gave him that over-the-shoulder look again, and now it reminded him of one of the wild things he'd stalked with his cameras, watching him as he approached her comfort zone, wary and uncertain, not quite sure whether to be afraid. "There are an awful lot of things you don't know about me."

*I probably know more about you than you can begin to imagine…things you don't even know yourself,* Tony thought. But aloud he said indulgently, with all the confidence in the world, thinking no matter what she had to tell him, it couldn't possibly rival the bombshell he was about to drop on her, "It's all right. You *can* tell me, Brooke."

She nodded. Said, "I know. All right." Cleared her throat, sat up straight, looked him in the eye and said, "I was molested."

He couldn't have been more stunned if she'd hauled

off and slugged him. He stared at her blankly. The words she'd spoken had no meaning; they rang in his ears like the discordant clang of a broken bell.

She rushed on, filling his silence with more of those incomprehensible words. "Abused. Sexually. Raped... actually. When I was a child. By my brother—*adopted* brother."

He was—had always been—a man who respected, even revered, women. The very idea that a man could mistreat or terrorize a woman—any woman, of any age—was simply appalling to him. But *this* woman... and a *child*... He wanted to cover his ears like a child himself. Wanted to tell her to stop. He could feel the edges of his world curling in on him, shimmering... turning dark. And still the words came.

"He was older—ten years older. It started when I was fourteen—that's when my sister ran away. He'd been doing it to her since we were about...eleven, I think. Maybe even before that. I think I knew, but I didn't want to, you know? So I didn't tell anybody. Then my sister ran away, and that's when he...he turned to me."

*Why didn't you tell someone?* His mind, finally functioning again, shrieked the question, but he couldn't bring himself to ask it. It seemed too much like an accusation. Like blame. And that was the last thing she needed, he realized. She'd been blaming herself far too long already.

He didn't ask it, but she answered as if he had. "I didn't tell my parents, because I knew they wouldn't believe me. I'm sure that's why my sister didn't tell anyone, either. He—Clay—was their *son*. Their *real* son, you know?" There were tears on her cheeks now. He wondered if she even knew. "He would have denied it or else blamed us. I know he would have. My parents were very religious—the hellfire and damnation kind of religious. I was sure they'd disown me if they knew. My father would have, anyway. I think I told you, he never wanted to adopt us to begin with. I think he just went along with it because he knew Mom wanted a little girl so bad, and she couldn't—well, I told you about that." She cleared her throat, paused and then went on.

"So…finally, I ran away, too. In a way. I was seventeen when I met Duncan, and he was so strong, so protective…and I thought, Here's somebody who'll take me away from here, and Clay can't ever touch me again. So, I…"

"You married him." He heard the harshness in his voice but couldn't seem to make it softer. "Did he—your husband—did he know?"

She nodded and brushed absently at her cheek. Her voice became a whisper. "I told him on our honeymoon. He'd figured out I wasn't…you know…so I had to tell him. At first he seemed okay with it—sweet, even. Angry, but not at me. I thought. But then, when I got pregnant, he started acting so jealous, possessive, like he didn't trust me. He actually doubted Daniel was his child. And that's…when he started…"

"Hitting you."

"Yes."

"My God." He discovered he was shaking. Shaking with a rage that demanded violence, a primitive rage that wanted to smash, break, kill. He shook because what was required of him instead was tenderness. "Brooke…" He wanted to hold her, wrap her in his arms and stroke her hair and kiss away her tears. But in his fractured state, he was afraid to touch her. "You do know none of it was your fault?"

She nodded…drew a long, shuddering sniff. "In *here* I do—" she touched her temple "—in my grown-up head, I do." Then her chest. "But in here…I don't know. Sometimes there's this person in here, inside me, this little girl, and she feels…ashamed and dirty and scared—" Her voice broke, and a huge shudder ran through her as she gathered herself to flee.

He didn't think, wasn't aware of moving, but somehow he had her wrapped in his arms, with her face pressed against his heart. He murmured things… soothing things…sounds without words, and she began to sob like a heartbroken child. She fought it, though, her body rigid, hands clutching at his shirt, gathering fistfuls of it, as if she wanted to rend something—anything. And he held her and stroked her hair and shielded her face from the chill and the light with his hand, as if she were a small, terrified orphan creature he'd found. And he let her cry.

He held her until she grew quiet, and when he felt her stir and resist his embrace, he let her go.

She pulled away and straightened a little, fingers plucking at the sopping wet front of his shirt. "Boy," she said groggily, "do I know how to kill a moment, or *what?*"

He looked at her, smiling a little, too overcome with

tenderness for her even to laugh. "There will be other moments."

"Yeah, but…" She cleared her throat, sat up straight and wiped her cheeks with both hands, not looking at him now. "Here I was, all set to seduce you into carrying me off to bed and making love to me all night. Guess *that's* not gonna happen."

Laughter rose to his throat in a painful lump. He thought, *God, what am I going to do about this? If I hurt this woman, I deserve all the hellfire and brimstone You can muster.*

"Not tonight, anyway," he said gently as he stood and held out his hand to help her up. He smiled. "Although I am going to carry you off to bed."

Her eyes widened above the hand she'd pressed to her still-streaming nose. "You are not! Big as I am, you'd have to be crazy. Probably cripple you for life."

He slipped an arm around her waist, laughing. "That was a figure of speech. Although," he added wryly as they walked slowly together, in step, back toward the house, "I have to tell you, it doesn't do much for my machismo that you don't think I could."

She swiveled her head toward him, and when he looked at her, he saw that her eyes were dark and grave, and that she wasn't smiling. "Honestly, Tony?" she whispered. "I believe you could do just about anything you set your mind to."

He couldn't answer her. And again, fear and guilt were a painful tangle inside him. *Dear Lord…what am I gonna do?*

Like a proper gentleman, he walked her to her

bedroom door and kissed her. And although her fingers lingered on his chest and he felt the tug of her longing as if it were something tangible—a rope, a lasso around his heart—he said good-night and left her there.

"Sleep well…" he whispered as he touched his lips to her forehead, knowing he would not.

Brooke woke to sticky eyelids and a dry mouth and the feeling that she'd spent the past several hours at the bottom of a deep, dark well. Climbing out of it seemed not worth the effort—until she heard noises from beyond her bedroom walls and remembered. *I remember…moonlight, and Lady…and Tony. Tony… and me being a brazen hussy. Tony kissing me. Me… talking. Me…crying. Tony…*

A profusion of emotions, many of them in conflict with one another, nibbled furiously at her: shame and longing…fear and delight. Shameless longing…

She threw back the covers and rose, only to discover she felt as wobbly as if she'd been in bed a week with the flu. *What is this?* she thought. *Am I sick? I'm never sick.*

The noises she'd heard had become voices—Tony's and Daniel's—and they were coming from the kitchen. Curiosity overcame both physical and emotional weakness, and she pulled on jeans and a T-shirt, raked her fingers through her hair and tottered across the hallway to the bathroom. When she emerged a few minutes later, she felt marginally better, but also keenly aware that she'd overslept. It had to be nearly time for the school bus, and Daniel—

These worries carried her as far as the kitchen door-way. There she halted, transfixed, as if caught in some paralyzing force field. She stood absolutely still, bathed in warmth and light, and knowledge sifted into her consciousness like sunbeams. *Love. That's what this is. I love this man.*

The tableau in the kitchen consisted of two people and one dog, all three, for the moment, unaware of her presence. Tony—he was standing in front of the stove, and he was wearing an apron. An apron! Where he'd found it, she couldn't imagine; even *she* never wore an apron. Daniel—he was at the table, busily assembling his lunch while keeping up a revealing commentary on the personality quirks of his various teachers. Hilda—she sat at attention between the two but had eyes only for Tony, for reasons that became evident when he flipped her a slice of what appeared to be…

"Hey—Mom! Tony made French toast. With cinnamon. We had it with applesauce, 'cause it's healthier for you than syrup, and it was really *good*, Mom. Hey—is it okay if I take the last piece of chicken for my lunch? And we're out of bananas, but that's okay, because Tony said he's going to town, today, anyway and he can get some more, so I'm taking grapes instead."

Her son's words fell on her ears and rolled away like raindrops on feathers. Encased in her shaft of enlightenment and towed by the tractor beam of Tony's gaze, Brooke floated into the kitchen. She murmured absent replies to Daniel's questions and didn't think to scold Hilda, who knew very well she wasn't supposed to eat people food or beg for treats from the table or stove, and had, in fact, already slunk off to her corner, looking guilty as sin. Tony smiled at her, and she smiled back.

"Hope you don't mind," he said, hefting a pancake turner in one hand, a griddle in the other. "We thought we'd let you sleep in this morning."

"No—of course, I don't mind." She said it with a gasp as she grabbed hold of the back of a chair and held on to it, fully aware it was all that was keeping her from drifting on into his arms for a good-morning kiss. Which would be the natural way for a woman to greet her man the morning after they'd made love. Which they hadn't, of course. But they would…soon. That knowledge— that certainty—made her voice husky when she added, "That's…nice of you. You didn't have to do that. But thanks."

"No problem. Happy to do it. I told you—the sisters. I don't want you to have to wait on me."

And she got lost in his eyes and his sweet, sweet smile….

Blessedly oblivious to adult undercurrents, Daniel chattered on as he stuffed his lunch bag into his backpack, slung it over his shoulders and shrugged it into place. He brushed her cheek with a kiss, bumped knuckles with Tony, and went charging out the door, with Hilda on his heels. And silence crept into the kitchen, heavy with awareness and charged with tension, like a spring storm cell.

Tension sang in the clanging Tony made as he put down the pancake turner and griddle, rumbled in the grating sound of the chair as Brooke pushed it aside.

Then she was across the kitchen, and his arms reached for her, and when her body collided with his, Brooke felt as if all the forces of a storm were breaking loose inside her. The fury and power, the excitement and wonder of it filled her mind and took over her body, leaving no room for fear or questions or doubt. No room for thought. She only knew when his mouth found hers…at last.

She tasted of toothpaste, he discovered, and for some reason, he found that endearing. A moment or two later—or it could have been longer; he'd rapidly lost the ability to track time—he discovered she wasn't wearing a bra under her T-shirt. *That* he found not so much endearing as—not surprisingly—sexy as hell. Accepting the inferred invitation, he slipped his hands under her shirt and brought them up along her rib cage to cradle the sides of her breasts in his palms. And her gasp tore her mouth from his, and she buried her face in the curve of his neck and shoulder.

"Hey…" He whispered it with his lips close to her neck, just below her ear. "I thought you said you only turn into a brazen hussy during the full moon."

"Moon's still full out there somewhere," she mumbled from the depths of her hiding place.

He wanted to laugh, but her hands were busy behind him, untying the apron's strings…tugging his undershirt free of his waistband, and then the feel of her hands on his skin drove every hint of mirth from his mind.

Then he did laugh, not because anything was funny, but because the emotions raging inside him needed some kind of safety valve, and for a grown man, laughter seemed infinitely preferable to tears. It was soft laughter, low and breathy, but it shook him to his core.

"Brooke, honey," he said feebly, "I think it's time I carried you off to bed now."

"If you insist," she murmured, smiling at him, and her eyes, peeking from under her lashes, had a pixieish glint.

He did. He swept her up in his arms and was amazed at how light she seemed. Or rather, how strong and powerful *he* felt.

He was amazed that this woman could make him feel things he'd never felt before, when he'd known…well, quite a few women in his life. Every one had been special to him in her way, but *this* woman…*Brooke*… She was his birthday and Christmas, the most wonderful Christmas of his life, with an endless supply of packages, each one to be slowly unwrapped and savored, each one revealing something new and exciting and wonderful. Somehow he knew that with this woman, he'd still be finding new packages to open when they were both ninety.

The realization stunned him and tempered his passion with a tenderness and care he was sure he'd never felt before.

And didn't want to look at too closely—not then.

He carried her to his room—the spare room—not hers, and wasn't sure why. Some primitive instinct, maybe, that made him want to bring her into *his* place—a kind of *claiming*. And that, too, was something he'd never felt before. And didn't want to look at closely.

He looked instead into her eyes and lost himself there.

"I hope you don't think—" she began, and he dipped his head and silenced her with a kiss.

"I don't," he whispered. *This isn't a time for thinking, love. If I let myself think—*

He couldn't let himself think.

He wanted her. Wanted her as he'd never wanted a woman before. Wanted her with the finest nerve endings in his skin and the deepest marrow in his bones. But it was a strange kind of wanting, because he wanted not to *take* something from her, but to *give* it. He wanted to give her pleasure and joy. He wanted to give her happiness. And hope. He wanted to give her all the good things in the universe, tied up with flowers and ribbons, and watch her face while she opened them. He wondered whether he would be able to give her all those things…and then knew, beyond any doubt, that he was the only one who could.

All that was in his eyes when he looked at her, in his mouth when he kissed her, in his hands when he touched her. It was in the unhurried way he removed her clothes and smiled at her shyness and at her whispered, "Guess I'm not such a brazen hussy after all…"

It was in the way he gave himself over to her so she could undress him at her own pace, even though her explorations—sometimes shy, sometimes brazen—made his muscles knot and his jaw creak with their demands on his self-control.

Her skin tasted to him like ice cream melting in the sun, and smelled of old roses. When she tasted his, it felt like the most exquisite torture and the greatest pleasure he'd ever known.

He groaned—could not help it—and she whispered, "Are you going to have your way with me now?"

"I think—" and he could barely form the words "—you've got it backwards. You...are having your way with *me*."

She tilted her head, and her expression was poignant, eager and sweet. "May I?"

"Yes, love...oh, yes. Whatever you wish."

And so she straddled him and gave to him the gifts he'd wanted for her: pleasure and joy and happiness and hope. And he watched her face while she gave to him, and knew he'd never be the same again.


Sometime later, when the earth had righted itself and resumed its normal spin, and she'd become reoriented to her place in it; when they lay together in the tumble they'd made of the double bed, talking in sleepy murmurs of the wonders and coincidences of fate, Brooke remembered.

"You were going to tell me something," she whispered. "Last night...before I...ruined the moment." And her ear, pressed against his chest, felt his heartbeat quicken.

"Hmm...can't remember now. Must not've been that important." His voice was a lazy growl, and his hand never faltered in its silken slide up and down her naked back.

But just the same, she knew he lied.

# Chapter 9

"I have to tell her." Tony stared bleakly into his coffee cup, having refused Holt's offer to buy him lunch at the diner. It had been hours since the French toast he'd had for breakfast, but it—or guilt—still lay heavy in his stomach. "This changes everything."

"Yeah, it does." Holt stabbed at a chunk of the meat loaf special. "You couldn't have waited until all this was over to sleep with her?"

Anger lanced through Tony, driven, no doubt, by more guilt. "Look," he snapped, "it's not like I planned it, okay? Hell, do I look like the kind of guy who'd move in on his best friend's sister, particularly at a time when she's in dire straits?"

"I don't know what kind of guy you are, frankly," Holt said. "I just met you myself, remember?"

"Yeah, well…I'm not. Trust me." He shifted and added darkly, "Okay, maybe you shouldn't. *She* trusts me, and I'm not exactly being straight with her, am I?" He let out a breath. "That's why I have to tell her. Now."

Holt picked up his napkin and wiped his mouth with it, then reached for his wallet. "Hold off on that, if you can. Just a little bit longer. At least until Cory and Sam get here."

"No kidding—they're on their way?" Tony picked up the check. Even the coffee had turned sour in his stomach. "Where'd you find Cory? Sam track him down?"

Holt nodded. "He's been somewhere in Africa—the Sudan, I think. Covering the latest uprising, I guess. Anyway, he just got airlifted out a couple days ago by the 'independent security contractors' along with the entire U.S. embassy staff and their families. I talked to him this morning. They should be here tomorrow sometime." He raised his eyebrows at Tony as he slid out of the booth. "What? I figured that was *good* news."

"Brooke told me some things. About…herself. Uh… jeez…" The last word was mostly breath. Holt looked another question at him, and he shook his head. "Personal stuff. About what happened to her when she was a kid, growing up. Her sister, too. The reason she got married so young. The reason her sister ran away from home." He paused, and even thinking of talking about it left a bitter taste in his mouth. "Hell, Kincaid, do I need to spell it out?"

"Her father?" Holt's voice was soft and dangerous.

"Brother. He was a good ten years older than the

twins. An adult, anyway. And they were just kids when…it happened."

They left the diner, with Holt muttering under his breath what sounded like swearing and blasphemy.

Tony nodded his agreement with the sentiments. "Anyway, Cory probably needs to know, and I guess I'm gonna have to be the one to tell him." He paused, then added bleakly, "He already blames himself for what happened to his family—the kids getting split up. This is going to just about kill him."

Brooke had never been so late with her morning chores. It was nearly noon when she turned the chickens out of their house, and they clucked petulantly at her as they stalked past her and through the door. Several of the hens were already on their nests—sulking, she was sure. She cooed apologies to them while she replenished their feeder with scratch and made a point to clean and fill their water bowls with fresh water. She gave the goats, alpacas and horses a little extra measure of grain, and gave the horses a good brushing before she turned them out to pasture.

She went to say good morning to Lady, but the cougar stayed on her rocky battlement and refused to come close to the fence. "Are you mad at me, too, my Lady girl?"

The cougar's head was low and her shoulders tensed—her stalking stance—as she stared intently past Brooke, toward the lane and the barn and beyond. A chill went down Brooke's spine. Clearly, something had upset her.

She thought of the SUV that Rocky and Isabel's "cousin" had seen driving out of the back road, and the look on Lonnie's face when he'd said, "This ain't over." And she walked back to the house, feeling small and exposed and vulnerable, like a rabbit in an open field, sensing the hawk circling high overhead.

She found Rocky and Isabel just coming down the back porch steps.

"We were looking for you," Isabel said, and she looked anxiously at her husband.

They exchanged a brief glance, and Rocky said, "We were worried. Ever since my cousin told us he saw the SUV again. This morning he sees this SUV drive past your driveway, going very slowly. It drives down to the back road and turns in, then backs up and turns around and drives past your house again. He says it did this three times, that he saw. He says he thinks it was the same one he saw the day Duncan was killed."

Brooke felt her body go still, while inside, her heart pounded hard and fast, and in her mind, a little girl's voice whimpered, *Tony, where are you? Come back! I need you....*

Then the voice was gone, and the stillness was inside her, too. She said quietly, "Where is your cousin now?"

Again, Rocky and his wife exchanged glances. He cleared his throat and shifted nervously. "He is gone. He left this morning—after he sees—*saw*—the SUV. He is afraid because—" Another anxious glance at Isabel.

Isabel stepped forward and said angrily, "He's afraid because he knows the sheriffs are crooked. They are bad men, Brooke. I'm sorry, but Duncan was, too. They take money, from the…from people like our cousin, and then they tell them they must get more money or they will kill them and send them back to their families in Mexico in little pieces."

"How does your cousin know this?" The voice came from the vast stillness inside Brooke.

"He had a friend—Ernesto. They came over the border together. The sheriffs stopped them, but they didn't make them go back or put them in jail. Instead, they took their money and told them they must get more from their families or friends here in the United States. Ernesto told them he had nobody here, and they took him away that night. My cousin never saw him again. My cousin managed to get away, and he came here, to us. So you see why he is afraid."

Brooke nodded. She folded her arms across her body and rubbed at her upper arms to try to warm herself, but she felt cold clear through, anyway, in spite of the September sunshine. She said, with a calm that amazed her, "Whoever was in the SUV your cousin saw…I don't think he was after your cousin—or me. It's Lady he wants."

"The lion? But why?" said Isabel.

"He wants to kill her," said Brooke. And in her mind was the image of Lady crouched on her rock pile, a clear and easy target. "I don't know why. Maybe because he believes she killed Duncan, in spite of what the medical examiner says. Maybe he's just crazy. But if I don't do something, he's going to kill her." She looked pleadingly into her neighbors' eyes. "Will you help me? Please?"

* * *

Tony drove back to Brooke's place on autopilot. His mind was lost in a swamp of confusion, where dark shadows and deep waters held unknown perils, and anxiety lurked like the indefinable fears and bad dreams of children.

He hadn't known such anxiety since he *was* a child, and he realized he was feeling it now for the same reason he'd felt it then: because he was vulnerable. Overnight, it seemed, he'd come to care for someone in a way that up to now had been reserved for blood kin: mother, father, sisters and brothers. This woman and her son—Brooke and Daniel—had somehow become his responsibility and concern, and their well-being and happiness vital to his own. The realization made him feel warm and excited and happy in a way he couldn't recall ever feeling before, but at the same time it made his heart tremble and his stomach fill with a cold, hard knot of fear.

The first thing he saw when he drove into the yard was that Brooke's pickup truck wasn't parked where it usually was. The second was that Hilda hadn't come bounding out to meet him. The formless fear inside him coalesced and grew and threatened to become panic.

He got out of his car and slammed the door, leaving the groceries he'd bought sitting on the backseat. He called her name. And that was when he heard it—the sound that sent a chill shooting down his spine: the squall of an angry cougar.

He ran, and each footfall on the hard Texas soil jarred his head and his chest like hammer blows. She's okay.

She's okay, he told himself, without rhyme or reason for either the fear or the futile attempt at reassurance. A hundred what-ifs tried to crowd into his mind all at once and only created a nightmarish chaos in his imagination.

From inside the barn, from the point where he had a clear view down the lane to the cougar's compound, Tony could see Brooke's pickup, and that it was backed up close to the gate in the chain-link fence. And what looked like the lion's holding cage was sitting in the back of the pickup. And Brooke's neighbors, Rocky and Isabel, were standing beside the pickup, their attention focused completely on what was happening inside the compound. He saw no one else, no big fawn-and-white dog, no sign of a sheriff's SUV or deputy in or out of uniform.

With his worst fear unrealized—that Lonnie had come back for Lady and that Brooke was involved in a deadly face-off with an armed and dangerous deputy—and his heart more or less free to resume its normal function, he now felt it swan dive into his shoes. *Oh, Brooke...what in the world are you thinking?*

Having already halted his headlong dash, faced with the improbable scene before him, Tony forced himself to proceed now at a less panic-stricken pace. He strolled down the lane, with his thumbs hooked in his pockets, showing no sign, he hoped, of the fact that his whole body was vibrating with adrenaline.

"Hello," he called when he was within a few yards of the pickup, and two heads jerked toward him in tandem, eyes widening with alarm. He nodded in a friendly way meant to calm the couple and said, "What's going on?"

Isabel looked at her husband, and Rocky gave a shrug. "She is trying to catch the puma. She says she is going to set it free."

"Jeez…" Tony whispered.

Isabel gave him a crooked smile and said, "Yes, I have been praying, too."

Beyond her shoulder, Tony could see Brooke out in the cougar's compound. She was standing with her back to him in the middle of the open area between the fence and the rocky knoll, facing the cougar, who was crouched on top of the rock pile. And even from where he stood, he could see that the lion's ears lay flattened against her head and her tail was twitching furiously.

Having been acquainted with quite a few domestic felines in his lifetime, Tony knew a very scared or angry—and in this case, dangerous—cat when he saw one.

He opened the gate and slipped inside the compound, closing the gate carefully behind him. "Brooke, honey," he said, marveling at how calm his voice sounded, "what are you doing?"

She turned her head to look at him, and for a moment his heart stopped. *Don't turn your back on her, sweetheart—please don't turn around.*

Her face was streaked with dirt—dust mixed with moisture that was either sweat or tears—and her voice shook. "I don't know what's wrong with her. I've never seen her act like this before."

"She's scared," Tony said, and the lion screamed and cringed back against the rocks as he started across the compound to where Brooke was. *And that makes two of us. I'm six years old again, and that cat is looming over me, just the way I remember. And my sister's hand is trembling in mine….*

Then he was beside Brooke, and it was her hand he held tightly. "Don't move and don't make a sound," he whispered, without moving his mouth—or was that a memory, too?

She looked at him with tear-filled eyes and whispered, "Lady's not a killer. She would never attack me."

"She's a cougar, sweetheart. And right now she's operating on instinct. If you turn your back on her and retreat, she just might."

Letting go of her hand, he slipped his arm around her waist and began to walk her slowly backward. Out on the rock pile, the cat let out one more squall, then did that doubling-back-on herself maneuver, flowed like liquid amber over the rocks and, in a blink, was gone.

When they were safe on the other side of the fence, Brooke turned silently into his arms, buried her face against his chest and gathered his shirt in fisted handfuls. Rocky and Isabel were nowhere to be seen. Tony wrapped his arms around her and let his cheek rest on her sweat-damp hair, but he was in no way ready to let her off the hook for scaring him to death.

"Brooke…honey… What were you thinking?" He gave an incredulous spurt of laughter. "You were going to turn her *loose?* Lady's not feral—she'd never survive in the wild. You know that."

She pulled away from him, brushing furiously at her cheeks. "Of course, I know that. It's just better than…at least she'd have a fighting chance. Here—" she swept her arm in an arc that took in the whole compound "—she's trapped. A sitting duck. Fish in a barrel. I just don't want to come out one of these mornings and find her shot dead. Or worse, have Daniel find her."

"You mean Lonnie." He got his arm around her waist again and began walking her back toward the barn.

She nodded and sniffed, then threw him a look along her shoulder. "You heard what he said. He said he'd be back, and he won't wait for a judge's order, either. I know him. And when Rocky told me about his cousin—"

"What about his cousin?" Tony prompted when she paused as if she'd said too much.

She hissed out a breath. "He said he saw a sheriff's SUV again. He said it drove by the house several times. Slowly. I know it was Lonnie—probably trying to see if I was home or not. I think when he saw your car, he must have decided not to risk it. But that's not all." She paused again to look at him, and her eyes were dark with anguish. "Tony, Isabel said some of the deputies are involved in some kind of extortion ring. Involving the illegals, you know? A lot of them come through here, because it's right on the way from the border to the big cities, like Dallas and Fort Worth, but off the interstate, where most of the patrols are. These deputies, if they catch them, they make them pay money so they won't get sent back or put in jail, and if they can't come up with the money…" A shudder ran through her, and she threw him a bleak look. "Isabel says they kill them, Tony. She said Duncan was in on it, too. Do you think…could that have anything to do with why he died?"

"I don't know," he said, and it was the truth. He was

frowning, thinking he needed to get this information to Holt as soon as he possibly could, although he still couldn't imagine why, if Duncan Grant had had a falling out with his partners in crime, they hadn't just shot him and dumped the body somewhere out in the vastness of West Texas. He was also thinking he needed to tell Brooke everything, and wondering if this was the right time.

He'd about decided it was never going to be the right time, and this was probably as good as it was going to get, when Brooke suddenly gasped and said, "Oh God—Hilda. I hope she hasn't broken the door down," and took off running for the house.

Giving his heart time to settle back into a normal rhythm, Tony followed at a more sedate pace. He was crossing the yard when Hilda came galloping out to give him a lick and collect the fur-ruffling hug that was her due, then loped off to the pasture to see how the rest of her flock was faring. And he went on to where Brooke was waiting for him on the porch steps, drawn now by the tractor beam of her eyes.

"We shut her up so she wouldn't scare Lady away," she said, and the quick-time thumping of her heart and the hitch in her breathing made the words jump in an unrhythmic pattern. She pressed a closed fist against her chest and tried not to let her feelings show.

This *wanting* was new to her. Even without going further into her sexual past than her marriage—*no, I'm not about to go there!*—she'd never *wanted*, not like this. It wasn't that she hadn't sometimes enjoyed herself with Duncan, although not nearly as often as she'd pretended to. She'd even initiated the lovemaking once in a while, because she'd known it made Duncan happy when she did. But every time, when she'd known it was going to happen, there had been that moment of fear. That little clenching in her stomach, that flash of thought she tried not to notice because it seemed shameful and unnatural, and she dared not let Duncan or even herself know it was there. Just that teensy little, there-and-then-gone-again *no!*

But with Tony, she *wanted*. Wanted *him*, with a hunger that astounded her. Astounded, because it didn't embarrass her at all, but only made her want to smile.

Watching him bend down to ruffle Hilda's neck fur, seeing his hands, so dark against the dog's white-and-fawn coat, she hungered for those hands, wanted them touching her body again the way he'd touched her this morning. Was it only this morning? *It seems like forever ago. And how can I be so hungry for him already?*

Watching him straighten and come on across the yard, seeing his mouth curve in that honey-sweet smile, she wanted his mouth kissing her, kissing her everywhere, wanted it the way a starving person wants, smelling the delicious aroma of food. Juices pooled in her mouth, so that she had to swallow and lick her lips, and her lips burned in spite of the moisture she'd put there.

Watching him reach the bottom of the steps and pause to look up at her, seeing his eyes glow golden at the sight of her, she felt her body grow heavy and hot, and pulses jump in places still tender from their earlier union with his body.

She knew he was watching her, seeing her eyes grow slumberous and her smile seductive, seeing the way her nipples beaded in sharp outline beneath her shirt, and she didn't feel even a flash of fear or self-consciousness, not even a faint echo in her mind of *no!*

He'd come to the step below hers and, without a word, reached out and hooked an arm around her waist, pulled her to him and lifted his face for her kiss.

But she didn't kiss him, not right away. She took his face between her two hands and gazed down at him, stroked the broad planes of his cheekbones with her thumbs and marveled at how beautiful he was, and that just looking at him could make her feel so…*happy.*

*What did I do to deserve this? Especially now, when I have no right at all to be happy.*

"Are you going to kiss me, or what?" Tony said.

She gave a faint whimper of a laugh. "I was afraid it might be too soon."

"Hey, I'm a guy—when it comes to sex, we have short…mmm…"

It was all the encouragement she needed. She let herself sink into his kiss and felt her body grow weightless and her mind go floating off into a pale pink haze. *Yes…this is love. I…adore…this…man.*

She was barely aware when he came up to her step, then tangoed her backward through the door and onto the porch…then into the kitchen. There he paused to look into her eyes and whisper, "Your place or mine?"

"Mine…" She murmured it without opening her eyes, and they were moving again, and she couldn't have cared less where they wound up as long as it was together.

They undressed each other standing up this time, not in a frantic hurry, but not too slowly, either. When they were both naked, Brooke placed her palms on Tony's chest and watched her fingers fan on his smooth mahogany skin, and she shivered, not with cold, but with a surfeit of feelings.

"So beautiful," she whispered, lost in the miracle of him.

He lowered his forehead to hers. "What is, love?"

"You…your skin…your body. You are."

*"Me?"* He gave a little gulp of laughter. "Man, that's a first. I mean, I am many things, some of which I'm even proud to admit to, but *beautiful?*" He shook his head in a dazed kind of way and, holding her waist with his hands, took a small step back from her so he could rake her body with his eyes. "*You*, on the other hand—"

"Hush." She shuddered and slipped between his arms, brought her arms around him and stopped his words with her mouth. Then laid her head on his shoulder. "As long as I am to you," she said huskily, and tears seeped between her lashes. "That's all that matters."

She felt a ripple pass through his strong, solid body, and his fingers glide through her hair with the delicacy of a harpist coaxing beauty from the strings of his instrument. His lips moved against her temple. "You are…more so than you can possibly imagine. And…I'd like to make love with you now. If you're ready." He cupped her head between his hands and tipped her face so he could look into her eyes. "Are you ready, sweetheart? Do you want me? Do you want me to love you now?"

*Oh, yes…if only you would. Could you love me, Tony? Not just my body, but…me?*

She drew a shaken breath and whispered, "Yes… please."

And as he had given the reins to her this morning, now she gave them, and herself, over to him. To his skilled kisses and artist's hands that made every nerve in her body shiver with delight…and to his tenderness that made her ache inside with longing. He took her to places she'd never known existed, gave her glimpses of joys she'd never imagined, lifted her to heights of ecstasy that terrified her, then gave her release that seemed to go on forever. And afterward, she wept and couldn't tell him why.

She couldn't tell him she was crying because it had ended too soon, and she was afraid she'd never feel anything so wonderful again. And because she was in love with him. Loved him desperately, irrevocably, with all her heart and soul, and had no idea whether he might…if he could ever…love her back.

*I think I love this woman.*

It slipped into his mind while his guard was down, while he lay relaxed and spent, with her head gently rising and falling with the movement of his chest and her tears cooling on his skin. And once it was there, it seemed pointless to try and deny it. It didn't even seem as frightening as he'd always thought it would be. In fact, acknowledging it was an almost giddy relief, like finding unexpected rapport with someone he'd been dreading to meet.

The fact that she'd cried didn't surprise him. It wasn't the first time a woman had cried in his arms after making love. What did surprise him was the way *he* felt, which was not like crying, of course—because he didn't do that sort of thing, at least not very often—but rather so full of feelings he didn't know what to do with that his chest hurt. For a moment he wondered if telling her how he felt would help, but decided it would probably only make things worse. After all, she had enough on her emotional plate right now, the last thing she needed was to have to deal with the burden of some stranger falling in love with her.

Then he thought about what she'd said about him being beautiful, and the fact that she'd seemed utterly sincere when she'd said it. That she could think such a thing about someone—he had no illusions about this— as flat-out ugly as he was just about took his breath away.

Of course, she was beautiful to him—okay, obviously, she was beautiful to anybody who wasn't completely blind—but beautiful to him in ways that couldn't be captured on film or a digital memory chip. Was it possible she saw something similar when she looked at him?

*Could she? What the hell does it mean?*

A strange shimmering sensation had begun to dance beneath his skin, raising goose bumps just about everywhere, when Brooke stirred and lifted her head to say groggily, "What time izzit?"

He lifted his arm and peered at his watch. "Hmm… 'bout three. Why?" Then, before she could answer, he thought, *Daniel!* and went rigid. "Oh, hell. I forgot. What time does—"

"About three-thirty." She stretched languidly and kissed his chest. "Don't worry. Plenty of time. We could even take a shower." She looked up at him from under her lashes, and her smile was impish.

"Brazen hussy," he growled, giving her bottom a gentle pat. "Tempting…but you're forgetting something." He shifted her off to one side and sat up, then turned to look at her and smiled. He couldn't help it, given the way she looked lying naked on her side, propped on one elbow, with her head slightly tilted and her hair feathered across one flushed and tanned cheek, lips still swollen from his kisses… The camera in his mind went *click*.

He said gently, "There's a cougar cage sitting in the back of your pickup, remember? Are you sure you want to try and explain that to Daniel?" She lay back with a groan and put an arm over her face. He laid his hand on her flat stomach and stroked downward, chuckling when she gasped and squirmed. "Come on, sweetheart—upsy-daisy. Let's do this. If the three of you managed to get that thing up there, I think you and I can probably get it down. Especially since we have gravity on our side."

He leaned over and kissed her, then gathered up his clothes and left her. And deep in his heart, he was grateful for the distraction that had made it possible for him to avoid answering the question that had popped into his mind just before she asked him the time.

It turned out not to be too difficult a job, with the help of the ramp and roller bars she used to transport cages full of goats and alpacas in and out of her truck.

"When you're a woman alone, you learn to find ways of doing things that don't rely on brute strength,"

Brooke told him after they'd wrestled the cougar's cage back through the compound gate. She dusted her hands and paused to catch her breath. "Of course," she added, smiling at him, "I never say no to brute strength when it's offered."

"Just out of curiosity," Tony said when they were back on the outside of the compound and Brooke was locking the gate in the chain-link fence. "Where were you going to take her? Do you have any idea how big a wild mountain lion's range is?"

"I do, actually." As she so often did, she laced her fingers through the chain-link and gazed beyond it, to where the cougar now lay relaxed in the shade of the oak tree, seemingly without a care in the world. He saw Brooke's eyes squint a little and knew it wasn't from the brightness of the sun. "The truth is, I didn't know exactly where I was going to take her." Her voice roughened. "Just knew I had to try and save her from Lonnie. Somehow."

She threw him a look, and the wistful longing in it kicked at his heart. "It was my big dream. I wanted to turn this place into a refuge for big cats. We're crowding them off the planet, you know. I have the room. The part you see here, the house, barn, pens and pasture—that's only about five acres. I have another twenty over there." She made a sweep with her arm. "That's all mine. I could do it—thanks to my parents' will, I have the money—but I don't suppose it's possible now. Not after this. Especially if I go to—" She swallowed convulsively, and it hit him suddenly—not a little kick, but a wallop that took his breath away—what she was facing and how terrified she must be.

He said gruffly, before he could stop himself, "Look, don't give up. And don't do anything stupid, okay? Holt and I—please, just give us a little more time."

"Holt." She turned to look at him, still holding on to the chain-link fence with one hand. "That would be…"

"The guy I've been sharing a room with—yeah. He's—"

"Obviously not a traveling salesman." She said it with a hint of a smile on her lips, but no humor at all in her eyes.

Tony felt a sickening dropping sensation in his stomach. He knew it was finally here—the moment he'd been dreading, the moment he'd known would have to come. And he knew it was going to be worse than he'd imagined, even before she said the words, in a voice that chilled him to his core.

"So, who is he, Tony? And while we're at it, who are *you?* And why are you really here?"

## *Chapter 10*

The amazing thing, Brooke thought, was that she felt nothing. Except for a strange quivering in her stomach, she was numb. She remembered she'd experienced much the same sensation the day they'd come to arrest her for murder, so she understood that this was some kind of shock, and that it would wear off eventually, and when it did, the pain would bury her. She could only hope she'd be alone when it happened.

In the meantime, in the calm and unreal world she lived in now, she watched Tony's face, and it seemed to flicker and shimmer like the images on an old-time movie screen.

"I'm exactly who I told you I am," he said in a voice that seemed unnaturally calm. Then he paused, and his eyes flared golden for an instant before he closed them. "As for why I'm here…"

"Who's Holt?"

He let the breath out with a hissing sound. "A private investigator."

"A private investigator." The shivering inside her was spreading through her body, and she wrapped her arms across herself in a futile effort to contain it. "So, who's he investigating? Me?"

"Not exactly…"

"Who hired him? Was it you?"

"No! Brooke, listen to—" He reached for her, and she threw up her arms to fend him off and stepped back, violently cringed away from him.

"So, *what* then? Let me guess. He hired you to come out here and spy on me, right? Who put him up to it, the sheriff? The state's attorney?" Now her voice had begun to shake. The shell was cracking. She gathered its remnants around her as best she could and whispered desperately, "You better tell me, Tony. Right now. *Who,* dammit?"

"It's nothing like that. It's got nothing to do with Duncan, or what happened here the day he was killed. It's—" He ran his hand over his scalp, something she'd never seen him do before, and his face contorted with what looked like pain. "Look, it's complicated. Can we go someplace—"

"No. I want you to tell me *now.*"

"Brooke—"

"*Now,* Tony."

He reached for her again but pulled his hand back

before it touched her and jammed it into his pocket instead. He frowned, then cleared his throat, as if in preparation for a profoundly important declaration. "Okay. You know you were adopted, right?" He grimaced, as if in pain. "Of course, you do. Okay. So…what do you know about your birth parents?"

"Only that they're both dead. What's that got to do—"

"Hold on. I told you it's complicated. What about siblings? What do you know about them?"

"I told you. I have a twin sister."

"Well—" he whooshed out a breath…dragged in another…gave a small laugh "—actually, you have more than that. You also have a brother."

He watched the blood drain from her face. She seemed to sway, and she put out a hand to grope for the support of the chain-link fence as she whispered, "I have…a brother?"

"Three…actually." He tried to smile. Air seemed in short supply suddenly, and gulping it didn't help much. "The way I understand it is, you were all separated when you were children, after your parents died. You and your sister were the youngest, just toddlers at the time. So you probably don't remember at all. But your oldest brother, Cory—well, a couple of years ago, he hired Holt Kincaid to find you—the four of you. He finally located your brothers early last summer. He'd just found out where you were and was coming into town to see…uh, to talk to you, when…all this happened. He got here the day of your bail hearing."

He stared at her and she stared back, not saying anything. Her eyes were like chunks of obsidian.

He threw up his hands. "Well, jeez, Brooke, what was he supposed to do? He didn't know you from Adam. For all he knew, his client's baby sister was a cold-blooded murderer! Both your brother and his wife were unreachable at the time—another long story—so he called me, since I happen to be a good friend of both Cory and Sam's, and…so, here I am."

"Spying on me."

"Ah, hell, it wasn't—"

"It's just like I said, isn't it? This Holt person hired you to check me out. You gave us that lion story so we'd let you get close to us. You lied to me, Tony. You lied to Daniel. That whole thing about saving Lady—we *trusted* you. *I* trusted you." She made a wide sweep with her arm, one that took in the dog, who was napping, oblivious, in the shade of the pickup truck. "Even Hilda trusted you. I gave you my—" And now the gesture she made was small, a brief touching of herself in the general area of her heart.

Then she wrapped her arms around herself again and looked away. She was crying, tears welling up and pouring from her eyes in a way that was all the more devastating by being utterly silent. To Tony, watching in helpless anguish, it was as if her very soul was bleeding.

"Brooke," he whispered, "it wasn't like that. We—Holt and I—we just wanted to help you. Lord knows, I never meant—" *To fall in love with you.*

There—he'd said it. Only in his mind, but still. He'd admitted it, what he'd known for a while. Now, finally, when it was too late. *I love this woman. I love her child, too. And I've screwed things up badly and probably lost both of them.*

"Why couldn't you just have told me? Once you knew I wasn't—before I—before we…" The look she gave him, the hurt and accusation in those shimmering indigo eyes, tore at his heart. "Or," she whispered, "is that why you didn't tell me. You still think I'm a murderer?"

"God, no! Brooke, you know I don't."

"But that's just it—I *don't* know. I don't know *you*. I thought I did, but now… How can I ever know whether you're lying to me or not? How can I ever trust you?"

"I didn't lie." His voice felt like crushed rock in his throat. "Not about the important stuff. Brooke, I—"

*"No."* She held up both hands, a wall between them. "I want you to leave. I want you gone."

"Brooke—"

*"Now.* Before Daniel gets home. I don't want him to see you."

Something inside him shut down. A kind of fatalistic calm descended. "All right. Okay," he said. And walked away.

Halfway through the barn, he met Daniel, still wearing his backpack from school. When he saw Tony, the boy's face lit up with a smile was like an arrow in his heart.

"Hey—Tony. Where's—" And Daniel, too young to have gotten so good at reading catastrophe in adult faces, halted, and the smile vanished. "What's wrong? Where are you going?"

Tony wanted to rush on by without explanation. Pain was writhing and coiling all through him, and the last thing he wanted to do was break another heart. Then he thought, *You jerk—you brought this on yourself. You owe this kid. Be a man, for God's sake.*

So he paused, put a hand on the boy's shoulder and took a deep breath. "I have to go." He put up a hand to stop Daniel's stricken *"No!"*

"Son, I'm sorry. I haven't exactly told you and your mom the truth. She—well, I guess I've kind of screwed things up. So…I have to go now. I'm sorry."

This time walking away was like ripping himself in half and leaving the torn and bloody remnants behind.

"Mom! What did you *do?"*

Brooke straightened, brushing at her cheeks, and turned to face her son. He'd halted a few yards away, breathing hard, his face flushed and furious.

"Why is Tony leaving? What did you say to him?"

She gave a high, meaningless laugh. "It's not so much what I said…"

"Then what? I don't understand."

She put her hand over her mouth and nose, sniffed, wiped, then stuck her hand in her pocket and cleared her throat. "Daniel, um…Tony didn't really come here to do a story on Lady. He came—" she cleared her throat again and caught a quick breath "—to spy on us. On me."

He recoiled as if she'd slapped him. "I don't believe you. Tony wouldn't do that." And then, as uncertainty crept in, he added, "Why would he?"

Tears were welling up again. She shook her head. "It's a long story, Daniel. I can't—" But he was waiting, glaring at her, and his face had a mulish look she knew well. She brushed at her cheeks and said, "He was hired…by someone. Someone who wanted to know if I was—if I killed your dad. He was hired to come here and find out."

Daniel gave an impatient shrug. "So, he found out you didn't, right? So, what's the problem?"

"Honey, he lied to us. He's not who he pretended to be."

"He is, too!" He lifted his arms and let them fall with an angry slap. "So what if he didn't tell the truth? He was helping us. He's gonna save Lady, too. Tony's a good guy, Mom."

"Oh, Daniel. You don't know—"

"Yes, I do. He *is* a good guy. It's like I told you before. You just *know*." He turned around and started to run back toward the barn.

"Daniel! Where are you going? Daniel—"

"He can't leave. We need him. We have to stop him, Mom."

"Daniel, we can't—"

"Well, I can! I'm not…going to…let him leave. Tony…Tony, wait!"

Brooke stood still and watched him go, one arm wrapped across her waist, the other hand clamped over her mouth to hold back sobs. She watched him until he'd disappeared inside the barn. And as silence descended, she heard a faint voice, Tony's voice, somewhere inside her head.

*You also have a brother. Three…*

Oh, God—what if it were true?

It was too much, finally. Simply too much, on top of

everything else that had happened to her recently. She gave a desperate, laughing sob...then another, and another. Hilda woke with a start and came trotting over to see what the noise was, and Brooke sank to the ground and wrapped her arms around the dog's neck and buried her face in her thick fawn-and-white ruff.

*Oh, God...Tony...*
*I have brothers?*
*I...have...brothers.*

Tony was dumping his camera gear and duffel bag into the trunk of his car when Daniel came dashing up, face flushed and streaked with tears. Tony hadn't thought he could possibly feel any worse than he already did, but he'd been wrong.

"Is it true?" Tony went on loading camera bags into the trunk. Daniel slipped off his backpack and let it fall to the ground with a crunch. "Is it true what Mom said? That you lied to us?"

"About a couple things. Not the important stuff." Tony was beginning to feel a bit abused and sorry for himself, if the truth were told. After all, what had he done that was so bad, except try and help her? That was all he'd wanted to do, damn it. *Help.*

He slammed the trunk lid and turned to face the boy. "I should have told you guys the truth about why I was here, once I got to know you and...well..." He took a breath and gritted his teeth. Forced the words out. "Your mom's right to be mad at me. I'm hoping she'll change her mind. If she doesn't—"

"No! I don't want you to go, Tony."

"If she doesn't...I want you to know I meant what I said. I am going to do everything I can to save your cougar, okay? I wasn't lying about that. And what I said about you being able to call me anytime—I wasn't lying about that, either. You have my cell number, right? If you need me, or if you just want to talk, you call me. Okay?"

Daniel didn't answer, just stared at him with eyes full of accusation, betrayal, disappointment and grief. When Tony couldn't stand to look at those eyes any longer, he turned, got into his car, started it up and drove away.

He didn't want to admit how upset he was, or that his vision was a bit blurred, which might have been why he didn't notice the sheriff's SUV parked on the dirt lane, the one that marked the boundary of Brooke's property.

Brooke had dried her tears and was trying to tell herself she'd been foolish for shedding them in the first place.

After all, what did she have to cry about? How long had she known Tony? A week? Less? So he'd lied. Not exactly an unprecedented event in her history with men. She'd been an idiot to throw herself at him. What had she expected him to do? Turn her down? And how would *that* have felt?

*No,* she concluded, *you have no right to be hurt, and you have nobody to blame but yourself.*

*This, too, will pass.*

And so, she hoped, would the awful ache in her heart.

In the meantime, there were chores to be done... animals to be fed. And now that the commotion had died down and Hilda had gone back to her shady spot beside the pickup and Brooke was alone, Lady had come to the fence to say hello.

"Oh…you sweet, beautiful lady, you," she whispered, putting her fingers through the wire for the cougar to sniff, then lick. "I don't know what I'll do if they take you away… How could anyone want to destroy something so beautiful?"

Lady's reply was a rasping purr as she butted her head against the wire, asking to be petted.

In the next moment—less than a moment—the cougar gave a scream of fury and recoiled away from the fence and Brooke, one paw raised in defense and fangs bared in a fearsome snarl.

Brooke was on her feet, cold with shock and vibrating with adrenaline. "Lady? What's the matter, girl?"

Then she heard Hilda growl. She jerked around, just in time to see Lonnie step out from behind the pickup truck. He'd come, she realized, not from the direction of the barn and the front yard, but across the strip of live oaks, cactus and rocks that separated her animal pens from the back road.

"Told you I'd be back," he said, smiling.

"Lonnie—"

But his smile vanished, as quickly and suddenly as Lady's transformation from house cat to killer, became something evil and menacing as his eyes jerked and his stare arrowed beyond her.

"Mom!"

Her heart lurched, felt wrenched from her body. She screamed, "Daniel, go back! Call—"

But Lonnie was too fast for both of them. In one long

stride, he lunged past her, caught Daniel's arm and wrenched the cell phone from his hands. "Oh, no, you don't, Danny boy. Mama's boyfriend and her high-powered lawyers ain't gonna save that cat. Not this time."

He hurled the cell phone as far as he could into the cactus and live oaks.

When his cell phone shrilled at him from the sedan's center console, Tony thought for sure it was Daniel. He was smiling as he picked it up, thumbed it on and said, "Hey, D—"

"Tony—glad I caught you." Holt's voice, not Daniel's. "Thought I better warn you. Just got a call from Shirley—from the diner? She overheard a bunch of the deputies talking a while ago, this afternoon. Lonnie wasn't with 'em, and they were talking about how they were worried about him. Said he'd gone off the deep end over 'that damn cat.' That he was going to screw things up—not quite the words they used—for everybody. And they were thinking it might be time for them all to get out while they still could."

Tony swore, and Holt rushed right on over it. "I've contacted the feds. Told 'em they might want to haul this bunch in while they still can, otherwise they're gonna be gone, in the wind. They're on their way. So's Cory. But I think Lonnie might be coming to a boil as we speak, and I'm afraid he's gonna blow before they get here. You need to—"

Tony swore again and hit the brakes. Holt yelled, "What was that? Where in the hell are you? Are you in the *car?* Holy mother—tell me she's with you, at least. Tell me you didn't leave her and the kid out there alone."

"She kicked me out," Tony growled as he made a jerky three-point turn in the middle of the highway. "I told her everything, and she threw me out."

Now it was Holt who was swearing with everything he had. "I don't care if she just peppered your butt with buckshot. Get yourself back there—*now.* If that crazy deputy comes after her lion, you know what she'll do, don't you?"

Tony did know, and he was so cold and scared, he could hardly drive. "On my way," he said and dropped the phone onto the seat beside him.

But not before he'd heard Holt on the other end, muttering something that sounded like, "Gonna get my client's baby sister killed!"


"Why, Lonnie? Please…just tell us why."

Brooke stood facing the deputy and tried not to look at the gun in his hand. She had one arm across Daniel's chest holding him tightly against her, and with the other hand kept a death-grip on Hilda's collar, both for the same reason: to keep them from lunging at Lonnie and probably getting themselves shot. All three—she, Daniel and the dog—were shaking.

"Lady didn't kill Duncan. The tranquilizer dart did. The ME said so. Why do you want to kill her?" It was the only thing she could think of to do, the only hope she had. If she could just talk him down…reason with him…

"It was that cat's fault! It shouldna happened."

Lonnie's eyes darted crazily, in that brilliant, unnatural way she'd noticed before, and for the first time, it occurred to Brooke to wonder about drugs. Then his face seemed to crumple. "It wasn't supposed to happen like that!"

Brooke felt herself go still inside. "Lonnie, what are you talking about?"

His eyes darted back to her, and to her horror, she realized they were swimming with tears. "I told Dunk it was a crazy idea. I told him. But he wouldn't listen to me. He wouldn't listen…."

"What idea? Lonnie, what did you do?"

"It wasn't my fault!" He swiped at the tears on his cheeks with the back of his hand, the one holding the gun, then gestured with it toward the cougar's compound. "It was that damn cat…."

*Drugs,* Brooke thought. *Either that, or dead drunk.* For one moment she wondered if she could reach him in time to knock the gun out of his hand, but, of course, it was an insane idea. He'd still be able to overpower her, and what then? What would happen to Daniel and Hilda—and Lady—then?

"See, Dunk had this idea, how he was gonna show you were an unfit mother because of havin' a dangerous animal on your place. So he could get custody of the kid, right? So he was gonna make it look like the cat got out of its cage and killed a bunch of your livestock, and that would prove it was a danger to the kid."

"My God…" Brooke felt numb, couldn't believe what she was hearing. There was no sound from Daniel, either.

Lonnie went on. "Nobody was supposed to get hurt! Okay? He had it all planned. He knew you had a tranq gun, so if anything went wrong, you know? That's why he wanted me to meet him here, so I could be his backup. But then the damn stupid cat wouldn't come near the gate!"

"She was afraid of Duncan," Brooke said softly, but Lonnie didn't seem to hear her.

"So then Dunk, he decides to go in the cage and chase the cat over here. He had a key to the gate. But he thought she'd be afraid of the gun, so he gave it to me and told me to cover him. We'd left our service weapons in the vehicles—couldn't shoot the cat with department issue weapons, figured that would raise up too many questions, kind of defeat the whole purpose, you know? So anyway—" he gestured again with the gun "—Dunk gets about halfway out there, out in the middle of the pen, and the cat's up there on those rocks, there, and she starts screamin', making that god-awful sound. And Dunk just stops in his tracks. Like he was frozen."

"Dad was afraid of Lady," Daniel said, and Brooke marveled at how calm, how grown-up he sounded.

"Yeah, well…he shoulda been." Lonnie sniffed loudly and wiped his nose with the back of his gun hand. "The cat was starin' down at him, like she was gonna jump him, and he started backin' up, and next thing I know, he's runnin' back toward the gate, and the cat's runnin' after him, and Dunk's yellin' at me, 'Shoot it! Shoot it, dammit!'"

Lonnie was pacing up and down now, back and forth in front of the fence.

"Only I can't shoot, because Dunk's in my line of fire, see? Then—it all happened so fast. One minute Dunk's zigzaggin', so I figure I've got a clear shot, and the next minute he's lookin' at me, and he's got a damn dart stickin' out of his neck. And he's yellin' at me, why'd I shoot him instead of the cat? And I'm yellin' at him why'd he zig back into the line of fire, and…the next minute his knees are bucklin' up, and he's down on the ground, kind of flopping and flailing his arms around. And before I could do a thing, that cat was right on top of him, and she grabs ahold of his shoulder. Like this." He demonstrated, clutching himself at the bend of his neck and shoulder. "I got the tranq gun up, but before I could get off another shot, the cat takes off back up into those rocks. So, I went over to see about Dunk, see how bad the cat got him, and…he's just lyin' there, starin' up at the sky, and he's not breathin'!"

"So you…you just *left* him there?" Brooke had never felt such rage. She could feel Daniel's body shaking with sobs. Tears were running down her cheeks, too, but she barely knew it.

Lonnie's face contorted with anguish. "No! 'Course I didn't. I—he was bleedin'—you know, from where the cat bit him. And then the blood quit comin', and I knew his heart had stopped, so I started CPR, you know? But it wasn't any use. I could see that, and I figured you were gonna be comin' home any minute, so I took the tranq gun and got the hell outa there. Well, hell, Brooke, I couldn't leave it behind, could I? Not with my prints all over it."

"So you left Duncan there for Daniel to find. And for

me to get blamed for killing him. My God, Lonnie, how could you? He was your *friend.*"

He waved his arms wildly, crying again. "Well, hell, how do you think *I* feel? He was like my brother, had been since we were in first grade. It wouldna happened if that freakin' cat hadn't come after him like she done. What was I s'posed to do, Brooke? You tell me. What was I gonna do?"

## Chapter 11

Brooke never knew what she might have answered. She never got the chance.

In the next instant she saw Lonnie's face change, his eyes snap into focus and harden as they looked past her. "I know what I'm gonna do now," he said, and she saw his chest expand as he drew breath. The gun came up, held steady in the lawman's two-handed grip.

She jerked herself around to look where he did, shot through with adrenaline. And there, on the other side of the fence, only a few yards from where they stood, was Lady. She had come silently, stealthy as only a panther on the hunt could be. Her head was low, her shoulders hunched, and her golden eyes burned with a predator's stare...focused...intent...and aimed straight at Lonnie.

It all happened at once: Daniel jerking away from her, free of her grasp, his cry piercing her soul; his name, her son's name, ripping through her throat, tearing her throat like a lion's claws; Hilda's snarl as she lunged, breaking Brooke's grip on her collar; the clang of a heavy body hitting the chain-link gate; the deafening sound of a gunshot only a few feet away.

Then, in silent slow motion: Lady streaking off across the compound; Hilda staggering a few broken steps before crumpling in a heap of fawn-and-white fur; Daniel on his hands and knees, sobbing, scrambling through the dirt to reach her side; Lonnie lurching drunkenly, slowly bringing the gun around, searching for a target. And from out of nowhere, a big, powerful body hurtling through the air, hitting Lonnie with a flying tackle that knocked him flat on the ground.

Tony never knew how he managed to cover the distance between the barn and the cougar's fence so quickly. He'd never been a great one for speed—more the offensive lineman type than running back. But in the end, even what was surely a personal best for him wasn't enough.

Through a reddish haze, images jerking and shifting as he ran, he saw the drama unfold. Saw the man bring his arms up, and the gun clutched in both of his hands. Saw Brooke turn, and first Daniel, then Hilda throw themselves at the gunman. Then he heard the shot, and all thought stopped.

As he launched himself through the air, he heard a guttural sound, a bellow of rage he'd never imagined could come from his throat. He was a primitive being, governed by instinct and adrenalin. This man was his enemy, threatening everything he loved. He wanted to *kill*.

His body collided with that of his enemy with a force that knocked the breath from his lungs and carried them both to the ground, but he felt no pain whatsoever, only triumph, and a kind of primal *pleasure*. He felt his enemy struggling beneath him, and his flesh was in his hands, and he was pounding, squeezing—

"Tony—no—*please!* Tony!"

It was the only sound that could have reached him through the roaring rage filling his head. Brooke's voice. He stopped, breathing hard, and his hands went slack. He felt her hands on his shoulders and turned his dazed eyes to her.

"Tony, Hilda's been shot. Daniel needs us. Please, Tony…"

"Okay. Yeah." He shifted his weight off Lonnie, who lay quietly now, except for the sobs that were shaking his whole body. Keeping one hand planted between the deputy's shoulder blades, Tony grabbed first one of Lonnie's wrists, then the other, and brought them together behind his back.

"Get his cuffs," he said between gulps of air, and Brooke's strong hands were there, unhooking the deputy's handcuffs from his belt. He took them from her and clipped them onto Lonnie's wrists, and as he stood up, then looked down at the man on the ground, he thought he understood the primitive urges that had motivated his distant ancestors to take the scalps of their vanquished enemies.

"Tony." Brooke was tugging at his arm. He looked at her and saw that she was crying. "He shot Hilda. I need your cell phone. He threw Daniel's somewhere. I don't know where…."

"Help's already on the way."

And he was bending over Daniel, who was kneeling beside the dog's body. The boy had taken off his shirt and had it wadded up and was holding it pressed to her side. His hands, the shirt, and the dog's fur were wet with shiny red blood.

Daniel turned his face up to him, and it was tear streaked but calm. He spoke rapidly, breathlessly. "The bullet missed her heart. She's alive, and she's still bleeding. But it might have punctured a lung, 'cause she's having trouble breathing—see? We have to get her to the hospital *right now*."

Tony dropped to one knee and got his arms under the dog's body. "Okay, son, keep pressing on the wound, okay? I'm gonna lift her now…." He managed to get to his feet with his burden and threw Brooke a look as she stood hovering, eager to help. "I swear, she weighs more than you do," he muttered, and she gave a helpless whimper of laughter and clamped a hand over her mouth.

"We'll take my car," he gasped as he and Daniel began making their way toward the barn, shuffling awkwardly sideways with their shared burden. He nodded at Brooke. "You drive—keys are in it."

She nodded and ran.

Behind them now, Tony could hear Lonnie squirming and struggling on the ground, grunting with his efforts to free himself from the handcuffs. Tony discovered he no longer gave a damn.

It seemed to take forever to get to the barn. Then through it. When they reached the far side, they met Brooke, who had turned Tony's rental car around and was backing it up to the barn doors.

Once again, she was amazed at how calm she felt. As if, she thought, all the terrible things she'd seen and heard in the past half hour or so had been neatly packaged up and placed in cold storage to await processing. Right now she was focused totally on the task at hand: getting Tony, Daniel and Hilda into the backseat of the sedan.

Which was why she didn't quite grasp what was happening, at first, when a whole fleet of vehicles came roaring and bumping up the lane and into her yard, raising a cloud of dust. They seemed to be everywhere around her, and the setting sun turned the dust into golden fog, from which came slamming doors and shouting voices and the stutter and shuffle of running footsteps.

"He's back there," Tony yelled, jerking his head toward the barn. "He might be running, but I don't think he'll get far."

Then men were jogging by her as she sat behind the wheel of the car, men wearing dark clothing and carrying weapons, and as they passed, she saw they all had large letters stenciled on the back of their jackets.

"Feds," Tony said from the backseat. "They'll take care of things here. Come on—let's go. I assume you know the quickest way to the nearest vet."

Brooke nodded and began to maneuver the car

through the maze of parked vehicles. But when they reached the lane, another car was on the way in, blocking their way.

"Wait," Tony said. "Stop."

The other car, a sedan very much like the one they were in, cleared the lane, then pulled over and stopped. Both front doors opened and two men got out. The man on the driver's side was tall and thin and wore jeans and a gray, western-style jacket and sunglasses. His hair was brown, streaked with silver and longer than the current fashion. The second man was tall, too, though not as thin as the driver, and was wearing faded black cargo pants and a khaki-colored long-sleeved Henley shirt. His hair was darker brown, cut shorter, but also showed flecks of silver. He was wearing sunglasses, too, and he took them off as he walked toward her. And although there were tears in his eyes, he smiled.

She heard a small whimpering sound, realized it was coming from herself and clamped a hand over her mouth. She'd begun to shake.

*Oh, God—I know those eyes. Those are my eyes... Daniel's eyes. Oh, God—it's true, what Tony said....*

The man was bending down, looking at her through her open car window. He gave a self-conscious laugh but didn't acknowledge or apologize for his tears as he said huskily, "Hello, Brooke... You don't know me, but I'm your brother Cory."

She nodded and let go a sob...a laugh...both mixed together.

"The other guy is Holt," said Tony from the backseat.

"And I hate like hell to spoil the family reunion, but, uh…we've got a wounded hero here…."

And Daniel, kneeling on the floor, with his hands pressing the bloody shirt against the dog's side, added his breathless, "Yeah, Mom, can we go—please?"

Holt reached around Cory to open Brooke's door. "I'll drive. Mr. Pearson, if you'll ride shotgun…"

Cory nodded, and she felt his hand on her elbow as he helped her out of the car. He opened the back door and she slid onto the seat beside Tony.

"Tell us where to go—we'll get you there," he said softly, bending down to look into her eyes.

*He has such kind eyes. Daniel's eyes.* She nodded, and he straightened up and slammed the door. A moment later he was climbing into the front seat and Holt put the car in gear and they were off.

"Left at the road," she called and felt something stir against her thigh. She looked down and saw Hilda trying to lick her hand. Tenderly, she lifted the great shaggy head onto her thigh and burrowed her fingers deep into the dog's white neck ruff. Her vision blurred.

"She's so protective of us," she whispered.

"Yeah," said Daniel. "She saved Lady's life. I didn't even know she *liked* Lady."

Brooke gave a teary spurt of laughter, and Tony said gruffly, "It was your life she was trying to save, son, and if you ever do such a dumb thing again, your mom ought to skin you alive."

She turned her head to look at him, and the tears in her eyes spilled over and ran down her cheeks. "Tony,

I'm so sorry. This was my fault." Her voice was a very small squeak.

He shook his head and started to say something, to protest, tell her none of it was in any way, shape or form her fault, that he was the rotter who'd bungled things from the beginning. But she plunged on.

"I was stupid. Childish. I shouldn't have told you… what I told you. He was—he came from the back road. Right after you left. I think he was just waiting for you to leave. If I hadn't—" She jerked her attention back to the road ahead. "Oh—right at the stop sign." She drew a shaking breath. "If I hadn't made you leave—"

"He would have come for the lion sooner or later," Holt said as he made the turn on screeching tires. "And chances are it would have ended up worse than it did."

Tony got his arm around Brooke's shoulders and drew her against him. "The only thing I can't figure," he said as she laid her head down on his shoulder and he kissed the top of her head, "is *why*."

Brooke's head popped up, and she looked at him with eyes wide and dark. "Oh—that's right! You weren't there. You didn't hear him. It was Lonnie. He killed Duncan. But it was an accident. He never meant—"

"It was my fault." Daniel's voice was soft and husky. His head was bowed, but Tony caught the silvery flash of a tear as it fell. "The whole reason Dad got killed is because of me. 'Cause he wanted me to live with him, and I told him I didn't want to, and I was gonna tell the judge that, too. So he tried to make it so I'd *have* to go and live with him, no matter what. And that's why he's dead."

For a few seconds, there was absolute silence in the car. Brooke had her eyes closed and her hand clamped over her mouth. Tony was thinking how wrong the kid was on so many different levels, and trying to figure out how to say it in a way the child would believe. Then Cory shifted around, reached over the back of the seat and laid his hand on Daniel's head.

"Son, believe me, I know how you feel. I spent most of my life feeling certain the terrible things that had happened to people I loved were my fault." He spoke to the boy, but his eyes were on Brooke, and she opened hers and looked back at him. The two pairs of eyes, so much alike, clung to each other with such intensity, it seemed an almost *touchable* bond connected the two of them. Watching, Tony felt an ache in his throat and a knot in his chest roughly the size of a baseball.

Cory went on, speaking in a voice that was vibrant with emotion, firm yet quiet. The kind of voice that can banish a child's nightmares. "It's taken me most of my life to realize that it's the mistakes and bad choices adults make that cause terrible things to happen to children, and that most of the time there's not a darn thing the children can do about it. Except survive. Be strong." He paused to smile at his sister, a smile of such sadness and regret, it was hard to look at, but one filled at the same time with such love and joy, Tony couldn't look away. "I'm telling you this now because I didn't have anyone to tell it to me when I was your age and in your shoes. If I had, maybe I'd have been able to come looking for you a lot sooner. I might have found you years ago."

"But then, if you had," said Brooke, smiling at her brother, giving him the same heartbreakingly radiant smile, "I wouldn't have Daniel." She turned the smile on Tony and whispered, "Or you."

Tony saw Cory's eyebrows shoot up, and he gave his best friend a shrug and a shaken laugh. "Yeah," he growled as he drew his woman's head back down into its nest just over his heart, and then he closed his eyes.

And into his mind came the image of a cougar's tawny face, with its black mask and glowing yellow eyes…the image of his own childhood nightmares. He thought then about what his Apache grandmother had told him of spirit messengers, and wondered whether there might be something to that stuff, after all.

"Uh…guys? Brooke?" Holt's gravelly voice came from the front seat. "Am I supposed to be turning anytime soon?"


It was late, long past midnight, when they got back to Brooke's place. They'd left Hilda behind in the veterinary hospital, sedated and resting comfortably after the long surgery to repair damage to her lungs—Daniel had been correct in his diagnosis, to his great satisfaction—and also to her ribs and some other stuff, the names of which Tony wasn't sure about. Holt and Cory had dropped Tony, Brooke and a sleeping Daniel off at the back porch steps and had taken Holt's rental car back to town, to the Cactus Country Inn.

The waning moon was high and bright in a cloudless Texas sky, and it lighted their way up the steps of the dark house—they'd left it in a hurry and before sundown. Brooke held the door while Tony carried Daniel into the kitchen, then slipped past him and down the hall to pull back the covers so Tony could lay him gently down on the bed. Together, they slipped off his shoes and jeans and the jacket Cory had given him to wear when the evening grew cool, since Daniel's shirt was now somewhere in a biohazard trash can at the vet's. Brooke folded the covers over the sleeping child and leaned down to kiss him while Tony let his fingers linger in the boy's soft, silky hair. Then they both tiptoed silently out of the room.

Brooke pulled the door closed. And they stood in the hallway and faced each other in the darkness, close but not touching. They both drew breath and spoke.

"Brooke…"

"Tony…"

He felt her fingers on his lips, and she whispered, "I'm sorry. For what I said to you."

He caught her hand and held it. "No apology necessary." His whisper was much deeper and gruffer than hers.

"Can you stay?"

"As long as you want me."

He heard her breath catch. "Do you mean that?"

"I do," he said, fully aware that it was a vow.

He could feel her shaking, so he drew her close to him and held her, wrapped in his arms. Her arms came around him, and her head came to rest in its special place. He laid his cheek against her hair and drew a deep breath, breathing in the smell of her that had already become familiar to him. "I was thinking… about that dream of yours. About the big cats? Since it looks like you're going to be able to do that now, after all…it seems to me like you might need a partner."

"I will," she said, fully aware that it was a vow. She could hear his heart thumping against her ear, like a drum deep inside his big chest. "Absolutely."

They stood there like that for a long time, as close as two people could be, neither of them wanting to separate from the other, neither of them wanting the moment to end.

After a while, Tony cleared his throat and said, "I want you to know, you've made my mother and a whole bunch of sisters very, very happy."

She gave a soft laugh. "Yeah, well…Daniel, too." She tipped her head to look at him, and a tiny hint of uncertainty crept into her voice. "And you?"

"Happy doesn't begin to describe it." He managed to get that much out before words failed him completely.

After that, it seemed easier just to show her.

The next morning, Brooke was making blueberry pancakes when the knock came—on the front door, not the back porch door, which everyone always used. She left Daniel and Tony laughing over something or other and went to answer it, wiping her hands on a dish towel.

Sheriff Clayton Carter stood on her front porch, wearing the same Western-style jacket he'd had on the day he'd come to arrest her for murder. His brown Stetson hat was in his hands.

"Why, Sheriff," Brooke said, holding the screen door

open and smiling at him, "what a nice surprise. Would you care to come in for coffee and blueberry pancakes?"

The sheriff gestured with his hat and didn't smile back. He cleared his throat and tried to look her in the eyes, but his frowning gaze kept sliding past her. "No, ma'am—thank you for askin', but I can't stay. Just wanted to tell you personally, the charges against you are bein' dropped. And, uh…wanted to extend the department's sincere apologies to you and your boy there." He tried again to make eye contact, and this time managed to hold on long enough to add, "I'm sorry as I can be about your husband, ma'am, and I hope you can find it in your heart to… uh—" He waved the hat once more, then put it back on his head. "Well, that's all. Just wanted to let you know," he said as he turned to go down the steps.

"That's nice of you, Sheriff. I do appreciate you stoppin' by," Brooke said, and there was nothing in the world that could take away her smile—not today, maybe not ever again. "Are you sure you won't come in for coffee?"

With a wave of his hand, the sheriff went on down the steps. "Thanks. I 'preciate the offer, I really do, but I've got to get back to the barn. Got feds swarming all over the place…."

Brooke closed the door gently and went back to the kitchen. And was greeted there by two smiles, both so different, both so unbelievably sweet…and two pairs of eyes, one deep and dark like hers, like his uncle's, the other warm and golden, like sunshine…both of them lighting up at the sight of her.

Two faces glowing with love…for *her.* Two men— *her* men. The two people she loved more than anyone on earth, more than she'd thought it was possible to love.

As she joined them, she was laughing, laughing with a happiness that went all the way deep down inside of her, all the way into her heart and soul.

*Epilogue*

"I never thought it would happen," Cory said to Holt over steak and eggs at the diner. "Not to Tony. He's always been... Well, let's just say, he's somewhat of a lady's man. I didn't think he'd ever find..."

"The *one?*" Holt lifted one eyebrow. "Who's to say there's a *one* for everybody? Maybe some people just don't have *one* to find."

"Like...you, for instance?" Cory's eyes narrowed thoughtfully as he picked up his coffee cup. "What's your story, Holt? I sense there is one—probably a helluva one, too."

Holt smiled sardonically but was saved from answering as Shirley arrived, brandishing a pot of fresh coffee.

"Sure is somethin', about Lonnie and them," she said as she topped off their cups.

"Well, we owe you, darlin'," Holt said, lifting his cup in a little salute. "I don't think we could have gotten there in time if you hadn't told us what you heard."

"Yeah, well…" She took in a breath that strained the buttons on her blouse. "I'm just so glad they're okay— her and the little boy. Too bad about the dog, though."

"She's gonna make it. Thanks to you, darlin'."

Shirley gave him a smile with a wink and a wiggle as she moved off to the next table. Holt looked at Cory and found him smiling, too. "What?"

"Nothing—just that you're sounding more and more like a Texan. Time to move on, my friend. Which brings me to the question I've been dying to ask. What about my other sister? You said her name's Brenna, right? Where is she, and when can I meet her?"

Holt let out a breath and pushed his plate away. "That's…gonna be a problem."

"Why? What problem? You said the twins were adopted together, grew up in the same family. Surely they've stayed in touch."

"I wish that were true." Holt picked up his coffee and blew on it, stalling for time. But there was no way around it. It looked like he was going to have to be the one to break the bad news. "Mr. Pearson, I'm sorry to have to tell you, but Brenna ran away from home when she was just fourteen. Brooke hasn't seen or heard from her since." He spread his hands in utter defeat. "I have absolutely no clue where she is. Or even where to start looking."

\* \* \* \* \*

*In honor of our 60th anniversary,
Harlequin® American Romance®
is celebrating by featuring an all-American
male each month, all year long with*
MEN MADE IN AMERICA!
*This June, we'll be featuring
American men living in the West.*

*Here's a sneak preview of*
THE CHIEF RANGER *by Rebecca Winters.*

*Chief Ranger Vance Rossiter has to
confront the sister of a man who died
while under Vance's watch...and also
confront his attraction to her.*

"Chief Ranger Rossiter?" The sight of the woman who'd stepped inside Vance's office brought him to his feet. "I'm Rachel Darrow. Your secretary said I should come right in."

"Please," he said, walking around his desk to shake her hand. At a glance he estimated she was in her mid-twenties. Her feminine curves did wonders for the pale blue T-shirt and jeans she was wearing. "Ranger Jarvis informed me there's a young boy with you."

The unfriendly expression in her beautiful green eyes caught him off guard. "Yes," was her clipped reply. "When we arrived in Yosemite the ranger told me I couldn't go anywhere in the park until I talked to you first."

"That's right."

"Knowing you wanted this meeting to be private, he offered to show my nephew around Headquarters."

So this woman was the victim's sister…. "What's his name?"

"Nicky."

The boy who haunted Vance's dreams now had a name. "How old is he?"

"He turned six three weeks ago. Were you the man in charge when my brother and sister-in-law were killed?"

"Yes. To tell you I'm sorry for what happened couldn't begin to convey my feelings."

The woman's gaze didn't flicker. "I won't even try to describe mine. Just tell me one thing. Was their accident preventable?"

"Yes," he answered without hesitation.

"In other words, the people working under you fell asleep on your watch and two lives were snuffed out as a result."

Hearing it put like that, he had to set the record straight. "My staff had nothing to do with it. I, myself, could have prevented the loss of life."

Ms. Darrow's expression hardened. "So you admit culpability."

"Yes. I take full blame."

A look of pain crossed over her features. "You can just stand there and admit it?" Her cry echoed that of his own tortured soul.

"Yes." He sucked in his breath.

"I work for a cruise line. Aboard ship, it's the captain's responsibility to maintain rigid safety regulations. If a disaster like that had happened while he was in charge he would have been relieved of his command and never given another ship again."

Rachel Darrow couldn't know she was preaching to the converted. "If you've come to the park with the intention of bringing a lawsuit against me for negligence, maybe you should." It would only be what he deserved.

"Maybe I will."

In the next instant, she wheeled around and hurried out of his office. Vance could have gone after her, but it would cause a scene, something he was loath to do for a variety of reasons. In the first place, he needed to cool down before he approached her again.

The discovery of the Darrows' frozen bodies had affected every ranger in the park. A little boy had been orphaned—a boy whose aunt was all he had left.

\* \* \* \* \*

*Will Rachel allow Vance to explain—and will
she let him into her heart?
Find out in
THE CHIEF RANGER
Available June 2009
from Harlequin® American Romance®.*

We'll be spotlighting a different series every month
throughout 2009 to celebrate our 60th anniversary.

## Look for Harlequin®
## American Romance® in June!

Join us for a year-long celebration of the rugged
American male! From cops to cowboys—
Men Made in America has the hero
you've been dreaming about!

Look for

# The Chief Ranger

### by Rebecca Winters, on sale in June!

| | |
|---|---|
| *Bachelor CEO* by Michele Dunaway | July |
| *The Rodeo Rider* by Roxann Delaney | August |
| *Doctor Daddy* by Jacqueline Diamond | September |

# REQUEST YOUR FREE BOOKS!

## 2 FREE NOVELS PLUS 2 FREE GIFTS!

▼ *Silhouette*® Romantic
## SUSPENSE

### Sparked by Danger, Fueled by Passion!

**YES!** Please send me 2 FREE Silhouette® Romantic Suspense novels and my 2 FREE gifts (gifts are worth about $10). After receiving them, if I don't wish to receive any more books, I can return the shipping statement marked "cancel." If I don't cancel, I will receive 4 brand-new novels every month and be billed just $4.24 per book in the U.S. or $4.99 per book in Canada. That's a savings of at least 15% off the cover price! It's quite a bargain! Shipping and handling is just 50¢ per book*. I understand that accepting the 2 free books and gifts places me under no obligation to buy anything. I can always return a shipment and cancel at any time. Even if I never buy another book from Silhouette, the two free books and gifts are mine to keep forever.

240 SDN EYL4   340 SDN EYMG

_____

Name                         (PLEASE PRINT)

_____

Address                                          Apt. #

_____

City                    State/Prov.              Zip/Postal Code

_____

Signature (if under 18, a parent or guardian must sign)

### Mail to the Silhouette Reader Service:
**IN U.S.A.:** P.O. Box 1867, Buffalo, NY  14240-1867
**IN CANADA:** P.O. Box 609, Fort Erie, Ontario  L2A 5X3

Not valid to current subscribers of Silhouette Romantic Suspense books.

**Want to try two free books from another line?**
**Call 1-800-873-8635 or visit www.morefreebooks.com.**

\* Terms and prices subject to change without notice. Prices do not include applicable taxes. Sales tax applicable in N.Y. Canadian residents will be charged applicable provincial taxes and GST. Offer not valid in Quebec. This offer is limited to one order per household. All orders subject to approval. Credit or debit balances in a customer's account(s) may be offset by any other outstanding balance owed by or to the customer. Please allow 4 to 6 weeks for delivery. Offer available while quantities last.

**Your Privacy:** Silhouette is committed to protecting your privacy. Our Privacy Policy is available online at www.eHarlequin.com or upon request from the Reader Service. From time to time we make our lists of customers available to reputable third parties who may have a product or service of interest to you. If you would prefer we not share your name and address, please check here. ☐

SRS09R

# ▼ Silhouette®

# SPECIAL EDITION

## FROM *USA TODAY* BESTSELLING AUTHOR
# MARIE FERRARELLA

## THE ALASKANS

# LOVING THE RIGHT BROTHER

When tragedy struck, Irena Yovich headed
back to Alaska to console her ex-boyfriend's
family. While there she began seeing his brother,
Brody Hayes, in a very different light. Things
were about to really heat up. Had she fallen
for the wrong brother?

*Available in June
wherever books are sold.*

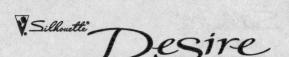

## MAN of the MONTH

*USA TODAY* bestselling author

# ANN MAJOR

## THE BRIDE HUNTER

Former marine turned P.I. Connor Storm
is hired to find the long-lost Golden Spurs
heiress, Rebecca Collins, aka Anna Barton.
Once Connor finds her, desire takes over and
he marries her within two weeks! On their
wedding night he reveals he knows her true
identity and she flees. When he finds her
again, can he convince her that the love they
share is worth fighting for?

**Available June
wherever books are sold.**

# Silhouette®
## Romantic
# SUSPENSE

# COMING NEXT MONTH

## Available May 26, 2009

### #1563 KINCAID'S DANGEROUS GAME—Kathleen Creighton
*The Taken*

Any time things get too difficult, Brenna Fallon runs away. So when private investigator Holt Kincaid shows up, wanting to bring her to her family, she buys time by asking him to find the daughter she once gave up. But when the child is kidnapped, Brenna must enter the highest stakes game of poker she's ever played as Holt searches for the girl, and both soon realize they're gambling with their hearts.

### #1564 THE 9-MONTH BODYGUARD—Cindy Dees
*Love in 60 Seconds*

Tasked with protecting Silver Rothchild as she revives her singing career, Austin Dearing must also guard the baby she's secretly carrying. As attacks on Silver become more intense, she's driven into his arms, and their attraction is undeniable. But can Austin protect Silver enough to keep their romance from crashing to an end?

### #1565 KNIGHT IN BLUE JEANS—Evelyn Vaughn
*The Blade Keepers*

Once he'd been her Prince Charming. But when Smith Donnell took a stand against his powerful secret heritage, he had to give up everything—including beautiful heiress Arden Leigh. When his past came back to threaten Arden, Smith had to emerge from the shadows and win back her trust—and heart—to save them both.

### #1566 TALL DARK DEFENDER—Beth Cornelison

Caught in the crossfire of an illegal gambling ring, Annie Compton appreciates the watchful eye of former cop Jonah Devereaux, but she insists on learning to protect herself. As their attraction grows, they dig deeper into the case, danger surrounding them. They'll need to trust each other if they want to defeat these criminals.

SRSCNMBPA0509